Clay Boy

Clay Boy

by Craig E. Sawyer

Clay Boy

This book is a work of fiction. All of the characters, organizations, and events portrayed in this story are either products of the author's imagination or are used fictitiously. Any resemblance to actual events or locales or persons, living or dead, is entirely coincidental.

Edited by Alyson Faye
Proofed and formatted by Stephanie Ellis
Cover illustration and design by: Elizabeth Leggett

First Edition: October 2023

ISBN (paperback): 978-1-957537-75-7
ISBN (ebook): 978-1-957537-74-0
Library of Congress Control Number: 2023943013

BRIGIDS GATE PRESS
Bucyrus, Kansas

www.brigidsgatepress.com

Printed in the United States of America

Thanks, Chloe, for believing in me and my monsters

Content warnings are provided at the end of this book

"Be careful what you conjure"

- Doctor Barry Tenzin Dorjee, PhD

One: Creation

1

The last class of the day had started peacefully, with the warm afternoon light wafting through the large window at the front of the room and into the dusty ninth-grade classroom, which still had the same wooden desks from twenty years ago. They were a combination of the '50s-style Munkegard and the '60s Heywood Wakefield desks, comprised of a steel base topped with finished plywood. The one that the boy sat at had the usual arrow-pierced hearts and demon skulls etched deep into its pinewood top. Up on the blackboard, written in red chalk, read: *Caleb Jenkins is a fucking weirdo!*

A grouping of sparrows had lighted just outside one of the classroom windows, and most of them scattered at the sound of the loud school bell, but one flew through the partially opened portal and glided to the high ceiling.

Caleb Jenkins grimaced at the noise. It was too loud. The world was too loud. He preferred quiet places like the patch of woods near his house.

He noticed the skittish bird, as the wave of his chattering peers poured into the room, but the others didn't. He was smaller and frailer than most ninth graders, with a roundish face and pale skin. A series of light freckles sprinkled over his nose and cheeks. He always carried a lump of clay with him. Teachers and parents whispered that his aunt and uncle were in a cult. His uncle, and adopted father Nestor, was a fire-and-brimstone preacher who held services in a barn just off the interstate.

"Hey, C-Caleb. This assignment is perfect for you," Mark Mallory said, mocking the boy's stutter. "What are you going to do for summer break? Let me guess, be really weird, and sculpt little clay statues to whack off to?"

His little band of followers, the Hyenas, laughed.

Caleb ignored the husky boy and kept staring at the frightened bird, while he started to mold the raw clay into the likeness of the sparrow.

"I know you c-can you hear me d-dumbass," Mark said, as he thumped Caleb's ear.

Mark's cohort, Eric Frame, a towheaded kid with bowlegs and freckles, grabbed Caleb's desk and shook it until the clay bird that Caleb was sculpting rolled off and hit the floor.

Before Caleb could pick it up, Mark stomped on it and smeared it across the concrete floor. This caused a churning heat in the pit of Caleb's stomach that moved into his chest until the feeling started ticking its way to his arms and head. Something was screaming inside his head, but his outside looked calm.

"Uh-oh, he's about to blow!" Mark said, which caused them to chuckle as they walked to their desks.

Caleb bent down to retrieve his broken creation, but a cheerleader with bright red-dyed pigtails, and way too much makeup stepped on it before he could.

"Great, I got this crap on my shoes!" she whined.

"Hey Lexi, come sit by me," Mark shouted to the snooty cheerleader. She was captain of the cheer team and was the female counterpart to Mark Mallory. They had been going steady for the past few months and were inseparable.

A pouty-faced Black girl with red-dyed hair, combat boots, and goth style clothes bent down and picked up Caleb's mauled bird, setting it back on his desk. "Here you go. Don't let those assholes get to you."

"Th-Thank you."

"No problem. You're really good at that, even though this bird looks a little sad now, but I'm sure you can fix it," she said, taking a seat behind Caleb.

Caleb looked back up at the ceiling, but no longer saw the sparrow, so he began repairing his bird, but not before noticing the young substitute walking into the room. She stopped for a moment to survey the messy room and prepare herself for the circus. Caleb stopped sculpting and looked up to find her staring at him.

"Pubescent little monsters," the substitute mumbled under her breath, as she erased the words on the chalkboard. "Okay, listen up class. Ms. Cardin is out today. My name is Ms. Rathburn, and I will be your teacher until she returns."

"Where's Ms. Cardin," Lexi asked.

"She was involved in some sort of accident, but I wasn't given any details."

The class seemed to ignore Rathburn for the most part.

"Should we close that window, so the air-conditioning can cool this room?" she said, but no one acknowledged her.

"Don't you all answer me at once," she said, and stomped over to the thick-paned window behind her and attempted to crank the lever that raised one-half of the glass, but it was proving impossibly hard to do. She broke a nail in the process.

"Dammit! Is this window broken?"

The students continued to ignore her.

Caleb always had thought that the art room smelled like mildew and melted crayons, A row of fluorescent wands hung in rows across the water-damaged ceiling tiles, just above the desks. The one above his head fluttered. He eyed the sparrow that had lighted just above the light in the ice-cube tray structure that held the glowing wands.

The substitute gave up on trying to close the window.

"Okay, I need everyone to pair up with an art buddy, and please wait to be told your assignment," the substitute called above the roar.

Caleb got along with most of his teachers, but this was the first time he had met the substitute, Tina Rathburn. She had once been the *Wheeler's Cove Baseball Diamond Queen*. It was a corny yet prestigious accolade in their small community. It instantly made its Homecoming winner a local celebrity for the time they held the cheesy honor and allowed them free limeades at the local Sonic drive-in and free movies at the Oldster Theater on Friday nights.

Students shot spitballs. Cellphones were being used under desks.

"This is such bullshit," Tina the substitute said under her breath. She put down the attendance ledger to apply more blush and fix her overly teased hair.

The students sat down with their chosen art partners, but two of them had no partner: the new girl and Caleb.

"Okay, you're going to choose something to sculpt. Oh, maybe I should finish roll call, so please wait until that's complete."

"When is Ms. Cardin coming back?" a buck-toothed girl in the front row asked.

"I'm not sure when she'll be back," Ms. Rathburn said.

"Okay, class, we have a special theme today."

The kids got louder.

Caleb squirmed in his seat.

Mark rolled a piece of paper and shot a dripping spitball at the back of Caleb's head. "Bull's-eye!"

Caleb didn't flinch and kept working with the clay. He glanced up to see Mallory high-fiving Eric. Caleb imagined picking up a nearby pencil and sticking it through the kid's eye. The thought frightened him, but the sound of the Hyenas was becoming too much.

"Please, everyone quiet down! I need to tell you your assignment," Ms. Rathburn yelled, her voice becoming hoarse.

Another spitball from Mallory nailed Caleb in the back of the head.

"Damn, no wonder I'm the starting pitcher," Mallory bragged.

"Bet!" Eric added as they gave each other high-fives.

"Caleb Jenkins!" Ms. Rathburn yelled.

The oblivious boy continued to work with his lump of clay.

"Hey, the sub is talking to you!" Mark Mallory said, and smacked Caleb in the back of the head.

"U-uh, me?" Caleb asked.

"Uh … me?" Mark mocked. "Yeah, she's talking to you."

The class snickered.

Caleb looked like a scared puppy.

"Yes, I'm talking to you, Mr. Jenkins!"

"Huh?" he asked, eyes darting up and down.

"You started working on the assignment before I told you what the lesson was."

"Ms. C-Cardin always let me start when I got here," Caleb said, barely audible over the noise in the room.

"Well, I'm not Ms. Cardin," she said.

"*Clay Boy* don't don't l-listen," Eric Frame said.

"Why do you all call him that?" Ms. Rathburn asked.

"He always has clay with him," said the buck-toothed girl, teacher's pet. "He needs it for his therapy."

"Therapy?"

"He's a little psycho who saw his druggie mommy murdered when he was a baby," Mark said.

Caleb glared at Mark. "D … don't say that!"

"Or what weirdo?"

"I … I'm gonna hurt you."

This was out of character for the normally quiet boy, and Mark Mallory could feel the eyes from the other kids on him waiting for how he was going to respond.

"We'll see who gets hurt after school."

"Okay, that's enough!" The substitute said. "Please, sit back down. I also didn't say to sculpt a bird. You should wait for the teacher to tell you the assignment."

"You mean *substitute*, don't ya?" A bored female voice piped up from the back of the room. It belonged to the new goth girl.

"Who said that?" Ms. Rathburn asked, standing to scan the back of the room.

"You're like what a security guard at a grocery store is to a real policeman," the voice added.

"Uh, well, aren't you rude, Miss—"

"Helen."

"Well, this is *my* class."

"Just go easy on him," the girl said.

"I don't see a Helen on my attendance ledger."

"Helen Darter. I just transferred from my other school," she said with a perfect eye roll and a touch of sarcasm. She could have been a contender for the most popular girl in the school, but she deliberately dressed in all black down to her scuffed-up Doc Martens.

Eric Frame pulled out his cellphone and started to video the exchange.

"You're not gonna find me on any list, because I just transferred from California. My dad is the new principal and baseball coach."

"Oh, you're the new principal's daughter?" the sub said, now with a brand-new tone.

"Ya got me dead bang, can't get nothing past you," Helen said, as she popped her gum. Her response was from one of her favorite '90s movies starring the late Brandon Lee.

"You're not supposed to chew gum in class."

"Oh, I know, Ms. Sub," Helen responded, with a chipper tone.

Caleb was staring at the ceiling, and that's when Ms. Rathburn noticed the sparrow.

"Oh, my god, is that a bird up there!"

"Ewww, I hate birds!" Lexi said, with a look of disgust. "They carry diseases."

"That's not true," Helen scoffed.

Most of the students turned their attention to the frightened sparrow, except for Mark Mallory who continued to torment his favorite victim.

Another spitball hit Caleb.

Thwap!

"Lexi, would you please go and get one of the janitors to come and kill it?"

"Absolutely, Ms. Rathburn!" Lexi jumped up and headed to the door.

"Don't k-kill it," Caleb said.

"Mr. Jenkins, since you have already started your art assignment, why don't you come up here and show it to the cla—" she tried to finish, but a half-sculpted clay bird came flying from the back of the room, hitting her square in the face.

The classroom was filled with nervous laughter and partial gasps, as they all stared in awe at Ms. Rathburn's bloody face.

"Oh, shit," Helen said.

"That's gross," Mark said.

"Who fhrew that?" the teacher yelled through a stream of bloody snot running from her nose all over her blouse and desk.

The students looked at one another, but the only person without their clay was Caleb. He had a distant look in his eyes like he was confused as to what had just happened.

The real sparrow flew out the window.

"Mr. Wenkins? Go to the principal!" Ms. Rathburn said, trying to stop the blood from dripping on the desk.

"I didn't d-do it."

"What, it just frew off your desk?"

"He said he didn't do it," Helen said.

"You can weave my class room too, Ms. Darter."

"Gladly, Ms. Sub," Helen said, before getting up from her desk and stomping out.

Ms. Rathburn slammed the bloody lump of clay on his desk. "You are in bweg treeouble!"

Everyone was staring at Caleb as he got up.

Ms. Rathburn held tissues up to her nose and blew out bloody snot. She frantically dug a small mirror out of her purse and held it up to her face. "Look at my nouse!"

Caleb picked up the blood-soaked bird on his desk and walked out the door.

2

Bill Hall was a giant of a man. A huge and lumbering human that stands right at 6'6". He was currently sitting in the back seat of a deputy's interceptor, huffing and puffing like he was going to blow some little piggy's house down. "Am I under arrest, Dwight?"

The deputy shook his head. "For the umpteenth time, no! You are not under arrest! This is just standard procedure for someone who finds a dead body in the woods." Deputy Dwight Greer looked like a mountain man with his beard and burly physique, but felt like a child compared to the Goliath farmer. Dwight had only been a deputy for a year or so, but it was better than his last job as a volunteer fireman. This county only had a bad fire about every three years. He was excited that there was possibly a real murder in the sleepy country town.

"You know me from when you were a kid playing ball. I can tell who you are, even under that scruff," Bill Hall said.

"Yeah, you been raising the flag for the anthem as long as I have memories of that field."

"You were a shitty shortstop. You could run all day and never leave the shade."

"Gee, thanks, Bill."

"I got things I need to be doing. Why can't the sheriff just call me, at home?"

"This will probably take less than an hour. He just wants to ask you some routine questions, so we can form a timeline. It's not every day we have something like this happen."

"Damn shame, that," the gruff farmer said, as he stared out at the passing cars. "Looks like someone choked the life right out of that girl."

"Can I ask you a question, Bill?"

"You're the goddamned deputy sheriff."

"You ever wear anything but overalls?" The deputy started chuckling. "I don't think I've seen you in anything else in my entire life."

Bill fidgeted for space in the backseat of the car. "It's the most comfortable thing a man can wear."

The ole farmer was known to be ornery and a little odd. The Middle School had given him a job raising the flag at the ball field for the singing of the National Anthem. They paid him twenty dollars and all the concession stand hamburgers he could eat. He would ride his lawnmower to the ball field, because his driver's license had been taken from him, due to his peculiar habit of driving down the middle of the road.

He was not always so estranged from the community of Wheeler's Cove. Something broke in the farmer after his wife went missing in the middle of a rash of murders that took place in the early two-thousands. Some had speculated she might have been the first victim of what came to be known as the Cove Strangler, but the wife didn't fit the killer's type. All of the girls found dead had been former Wheeler Diamond Queens.

The interceptor pulled into the small parking lot of the Frankfort Sheriff's Department, which had jurisdiction over the county, including the small towns of Wheeler's Cove and the even smaller community of Drecherd Hall.

The morning sun blared off the glass windows of the modest brick building that sat in front of a large field of cedars, with an 'L' shaped structure that contained offices and holding cells. Frankfort County only had one sheriff and four deputies. It could be once said that there were hardly no serious crimes ever committed in the county of Frankfort, but that suddenly changed, back about sixteen years ago, after the murders of several young women. All found strangled to death and left at the side of the highway. These killings went on for nearly three years. Four young women lost their lives, then it abruptly stopped. The killer was never brought to justice, and it left a bloody mark on the God-fearing community, a mark from which they had just started to recover, and now there was another young dead woman.

"I haven't been here since my wife went missing," Bill mused. "I-I'm not sure I want to go in there. Too many bad memories."

Dwight got out and went to the back and opened the door. "This ain't gonna take long, promise."

"Who's gonna give me a ride back to my house?" Bill said, as he stepped out and stretched, towering over the six-foot deputy.

The deputy rolled his eyes.

"Well, am I gonna get a ride, or not? I sure the hell ain't walking."

"I'll give you a ride back."

"Damn well better. I've got to feed my goat."

Dwight took a hard look at the farmer. He knew that he wasn't telling him the complete truth, but now he just needed to find out what the complete truth was.

3

Sam Darter was Wheeler Middle School's new principal and head coach of the baseball team. He had been an overachiever his entire life, but that feeling had begun to fade when he moved back to his hometown. The old insecurities of being back in the *Corny Cove* were still there, no matter what he had achieved in his life. Sam was lean and athletic, with a baseball pitcher's body.

He was looking through old newspaper clippings. The ink from the old paper bled off onto his fingertips. He had been the high school valedictorian and regularly made the cover of the local paper as a winning pitcher for his middle and high school teams. He remembered his father being strict and strangely jealous of his son's accolades, but his dad was a complicated man. His father became the town's sheriff while Sam was in the tenth grade. For the most part, everyone in town was fine with having the first Black man as sheriff, but of course, there had been some who did not, especially after the police began finding the bodies of young women strangled to death with their necks broken. They never caught the killer, which led many people in Wheeler's Cove to blame Sam's father for not doing enough to keep them safe. His father took that stress out on his wife and young son.

When Sam graduated, he received a full baseball scholarship to attend UCLA in California. He remembered the pride swelling in his mother and her disappointment when he left before earning his degree to play for the Los Angeles Dodgers.

Sam rubbed his arm as he remembered the doctor's words: shoulder surgery. They were the words that no pitcher wanted to hear. He made two starts for the Dodgers his first year and threw for six innings in total. He only gave up one run, no walks, and seven strikeouts, but the last game went two extra innings. He pushed his arm past the limit. A snap! The doctor informed him he had torn his rotator cuff and required ulnar collateral ligament reconstruction, better known as Tommy John surgery, but a little over half of those so treated regained their full pitching strength. The Dodgers dropped him like a hot potato.

He stopped placing the old trophies on the shelf and worked out his shoulder. The trophies didn't have the same shine they used to have. He turned to see a sheepish Caleb standing in his doorway, staring at the floor.

"Oh, hey there, young man!" Sam said. "What can I help you with?"

"I was told to c-come here by m-my substitute, Ms. Rathburn."

"Your name is Caleb?"

"C-Caleb Jenkins."

"Well, did you do it?" Sam asked, leaning back and crossing his arms.

"How did you know a-already?" Caleb replied, and touched the pocket that held the clay bird. It made him feel more at ease.

"So, did you throw the clay at the sub?"

"No. H-how did you know what happened?"

"Well, come in and sit down so we can discuss what we should do about it," he said, motioning for the timid boy to step inside.

Caleb shuffled in and poured himself into the only free chair in front of the principal's cluttered desk.

"Sorry 'bout all the boxes. I didn't realize I had so much darn stuff. It's amazing what a person picks up along the way. You guys are still using Tandy 1000 Computers. My daughter will fit in perfectly here!" He laughed. "She's like a devotee of nineties goth. It's a phase, I hope."

"I l-like her," Caleb said, still looking at the ground.

"She must like you too, 'cause she stopped by a minute ago to let me know that the substitute teacher was being a little too hard on you and she didn't think you threw the bird. I'll have a talk with Ms. Rathburn, but you'll have to do detention this afternoon. It's the policy of the school."

"M-my aunt expects me h-home for dinner."

"I'll call and let them know."

"Okay," Caleb said quietly with his head hung low.

"My daughter also told me you're pretty gifted."

Sam saw genuine excitement on the boy's face.

"You always carry clay with you?"

Caleb nodded.

"You like it that much?"

"It h-helps reduce my anxiety."

Something about Caleb reminded Sam of himself at that age, a talented kid full of fear.

"I'm trying to get more funding from the state for the arts, not just sports. Maybe we could have a show of your work in the gymnasium? Like, what would you call it, an artapalooza?"

The boy's eyes lit up. "Really?"

"Sure, why not? First, let's try and avoid getting into trouble and being sent to the principal's office. Deal?"

Caleb nodded.

"Do you play baseball? You look like you'd make a good third baseman."

"I am not g-good at s-sports."

"It's more than just being good, it's about teamwork and building self-esteem. Plus, I need a third baseman. I lost a lot of key players after graduation. You'd be doing me a big favor, and I'll return that favor with a school art show featuring your work."

"I do not think my a-aunt and u-uncle will let me."

Caleb pulled on his hair and looked around. Sam could see that the boy was nervous when it came to his aunt and uncle. He, too, knew what it was like to grow up in a tense household.

"Tell you what, let me talk to them about that. You just plan on coming to practice on Monday, after school. Deal?"

"Deal." Caleb got up and headed for the door, but stopped and turned. "I don't have a glove."

"Oh, wait a minute!" Sam reached into a large sports bag near the wall and pulled out a fresh new mitt. "Here," he said, punching the inside of the leather mitt over and over with a baseball he'd lifted from his desk. "And take this ball too. I always keep one inside a new mitt. Keeps the pocket broke in."

He tossed it over to Caleb, who caught it awkwardly.

"See? You can catch it! Ya know, that ball was from the first time I struck out a batter in my first game during my rookie year. Well, my only year."

Caleb smiled at the prize ball.

"Now get out of here, and I'll call your aunt and uncle in a bit."

"Th-Thank you."

"You're welcome. Now you better head to the library for detention."

Sam smiled and shook his head as Caleb ran out the door, amused by the boy's excitement. He took a sip from a lukewarm coffee and fired up his computer. He clicked on a folder entitled *Wheeler Middle Student Body.*

4

The screen filled with a list of the names of every student. He went through dozens of names and eventually stopped at Jenkins, Caleb H.

"Jesus, this kid has been to an army of doctors," he said as he scrolled down the sub-files, opening up one of many recent psychiatric evaluations: *99345 Evaluation & Management (E/M)* by Dr. Epslem, 2020.

Office visit: Caleb Jenkins

Caleb H. Jenkins, an eleven-year-old male, established patient suffering from depression, anxiety, and nightmares. Adopted by his aunt and uncle at one year of age after witnessing the murder of Claire Conroy, his biological mother in 2009. Aunt, Lois Jenkins, reports the patient has suffered from nightmares since age four, though he has no waking memories of the incident.

Sam took another sip from his coffee mug and cleared his throat. Before reading Dr Epslem's report he hadn't realized Caleb's aunt was the sister of the murdered woman back when his father became sheriff. He continued reading:

Speech: Severe stutter

Problem 1: ADHD
Comment: Relatively stable; mild symptoms

Plan: Renew stimulant script and increase the dose, if needed. Clay therapy to reduce anxiety. Have suggested a return visit in two months.

Problem 2: Patient displays social awkwardness, difficulty understanding jokes or sarcasm, challenges making or keeping friends, avoids eye contact. Possible Asperger Syndrome (ASD).

Comment: Seems to slip away from reality during stressful situations. Parents are concerned that the patient is showing early stages of Teen

Dissociative Disorder due to being present at his mother's murder, but that is not my diagnosis at this time. Patient has also displayed aggressive outbursts at school and home.

Plan: The patient displays high function in the arts. Recommend he continue with prescribed medication and clay therapy, which allows the patient to act out hostile emotions and provide opportunities for gratification, achievement, and acceptance.

Principal Darter leaned backed from the computer, letting what he had just read soak in. He picked up the phone and dialed Caleb's aunt and uncle. The call rang several times before being picked up.

"Hello?" a stern female voice said on the other end.

"Mrs. Jenkins?"

"Yes, this is she. How may I help you?"

"My name is Samuel Darter. I'm the new principal and baseball coach at Wheeler Middle. I wanted to talk to you about your nephew, Caleb."

"We refer to him as our son," she said. "Is Sheriff Marcus Darter your father?"

"Yes, and I'm sorry about your sister."

"You were just a boy back then. It would have been nice if your father found her killer, but that's in the past, and God saw fit to send Caleb to us."

"He's lucky to have a loving family that would take him in like that. The boy has been through a lot."

Silence.

"Mrs. Jenkins?"

"Is he okay? He didn't do anything, did he?"

"Oh, he's fine, but he'll be doing an hour of detention this afternoon because of a disruption in art class."

"But art class is his favorite."

"I'm not exactly sure what happened. I read in his file that he uses clay as a form of therapy? That's pretty unique. I've never heard of that."

"Yes, it seems to have helped a lot. Clay provides him with a natural method of connection. It's helps him to express himself and control impulses of anger. One of his doctors suggested it. He had been doing so well, until now, but the good Lord must have special plans for him."

"The substitute teacher has a broken nose from a clay bird being thrown at her, and—"

"You think my Caleb did that?"

"I'm not sure what happened, but it's school policy that any student who is part of a violent act—in any capacity—must attend at least one afternoon hour. If I felt Caleb deliberately broke a teacher's nose on purpose, we'd be talking about expulsion right now, but it's not clear what happened; just that someone near Caleb threw a lump of clay and hit the teacher in the face. The teacher says it was Caleb and my daughter says it wasn't."

"Oh, you have a daughter?"

"Yes, ma'am. Her name is Helen."

"I hope you're raising her in the church?"

"I let my kids choose their own path when it comes to spiritual matters."

Silence.

"Hello?"

"I suppose each to their own, but evil abhors a vacuum, Principal Darter. It loves to crawl into an empty space and fill a person with doubts and mischievous thoughts. I suggest getting right with God."

"My mama took me to church every Sunday."

"I remember your mother. She was a good woman. It's a shame that she left us in such a way."

This statement affected Sam. His mind flashed back to an image of his mother pulling her homemade biscuits from the oven, and their aroma filled his memory. She always believed so much in her son. He wished she was there to meet his family.

"Mr. Darter, are you still there?"

"Yeah, sorry."

"I suppose if you feel Caleb needs to go to detention, then that's what he needs to do."

"Don't worry, he'll be able to work on his homework. I just wanted to let you know in case you had to reschedule picking him up."

"Caleb walks home after school. We live just through the small patch of woods by the ball field. He likes to walk."

"One more thing before we get off the phone, Mrs. Jenkins. I think Caleb could benefit from playing a sport. Would you mind if he came to our Monday evening baseball practice?"

"Baseball?"

"Yeah, I think it would be good for him."

"I'll need to ask my husband, and there can be no baseball on Sundays. That is the Sabbath of the Lord."

"Of course. Your husband is a preacher, right?"

"He's a prophet, Principal Darter. Perhaps, you've heard his podcast *The Miraculous Intent of God's Vision*?"

"Uh, can't say that I have."

"You should come to our church one Sunday."

"I'm a little busy with the new job and the move, but maybe."

"One should never be too busy for the Lord, Principal Darter."

"I'm sure you're right. Thank you for talking to your husband about Caleb joining the team. I think it would help him with making friends."

"Thank you for calling."

"Great, I hope he sees how good it will be—"

"Goodbye."

Dial tone.

"That was … interesting," Sam said with a chuckle.

"What was?" An attractive woman with green eyes stood in Sam's doorway.

"Spying on your husband, huh?" He stood and walked over to take her into his arms. Marie had been Miss Washington State once upon a time, but her brains outweighed her beauty, and she attended UCLA on a full scholarship. She and Sam met there and fell in love fast.

"What was *so* interesting?" she asked, between kisses.

"That was a student's aunt. She told me her husband was a prophet, and he could see the future."

"Oh, wow," Marie said, rolling her eyes. "I'm not sure what to say about that. Does he give lotto predictions? You moved us to the most backwards place in the United States, didn't you?"

"He runs a church out of an old barn that sits off the main highway. We saw the giant cross on the hill when we drove into town, remember?"

She shrugged and sighed comically.

"I thought you were kidding about growing up in a place called the *Bible Belt*."

"Yep."

"You talk to your dad yet?"

"Nope, and I don't plan to," he said

Marie put her hand on top of his, stopping him from clicking his pen up and down. "Nervous about something?"

"I'm glad you're here." He kissed her neck. "Helen and me have missed you these past few months. Thanks for getting everything settled back in L.A."

"You had to get to work, and I had to figure out my own job. And I think it was good for you and Helen to spend some time together."

"One thing I've learned about being away from you."

"What's that?" She purred, as he took her into his arms.

"I never want to be away from you for too long. This family is everything to me."

"Relax. You are not getting rid of me, ever. And, now you have your two lucky charms here you are gonna get to the state championship."

"Two more wins and we play last year's state champs at Homecoming."

"So, you've been lonely?"

"Yes, ma'am."

"Maybe we can remedy that?" Marie ran her fingers over his tie and the front of his dress shirt.

"In my office?"

"You use starch on this? Seems really stiff."

"I didn't have much time this morning, so I did a quickie," he said, letting his hands roam down her lower back until they squeezed her butt cheeks together.

"Quickie, huh? I've been bad, and probably need detention, Principal Darter," she said.

"The boy's parents adopted him when he was eleven months old, right after the police found his mother's body dumped out by the freeway on Halloween night. My father was in charge of finding the killer."

"Hello? I'm in the middle of seducing you and you're talking about a girl getting murdered? And once again—"

"You're right. Sorry, but maybe I shouldn't be getting freaky with my wife in the office so soon into my new job."

"Oh, you really want me to stop?"

They started to pull each other's clothes off, but a loud rap at the door interrupted them.

A petite blonde woman with huge glasses poked her head into the room. "Door wasn't shut, so I let myself in. I have your second cup of coffee, Sammy," she said with a thick southern accent.

Sam shrugged his shoulders. "Thanks, Mary Beth."

"Really?" Marie laughed as she pulled up her bra strap.

Sam adjusted his tie and swung open the door wider. He took the coffee and motioned her into the office. "Marie, meet my assistant, Mary Beth Hardin."

The office assistant looked Marie up and down. "Very pleased to meet you, Mrs. Darter."

"Yeah, pleased to meet you too," Marie said with an *eat shit and die* expression that she didn't bother hiding.

Sam sensed the awkwardness between them. "Um, we're gonna grab a late lunch. Can we get you anything?"

"No thanks, but don't forget, Sammy, you have a phone meeting with the head of the board of education this afternoon."

"That's right, thanks for the reminder," he said, grabbing his Wheeler's Wildcat ball cap and heading out the door with Marie.

"Sammy?" Marie said, as heat rose in her face.

"She's harmless, baby. It's that Southern charm."

"Don't you *baby* me," she said and rolled her eyes. "Where's our daughter?"

"She told me she wanted to explore the town."

Sam took his wife in his arms.

"You okay with this move?"

"It's different, but I'm up for it if you are. The big question is, are you okay with it?"

"Yeah, there are a lot of ghosts here," he said with distant eyes.

"Well, you're gonna have to speak with your father at some point. I mean he's the sheriff. He has a right to meet his granddaughter, and she has a right to meet him."

"You don't know how it was growing up in that house. Some things you can't forgive."

"You have to let go of that anger or it will eat you up."

5

Statement of Mr. Bill Aldous Hall, 62 (May 18th, 10:30 AM, interviewed by Sheriff Marcus Darter)

Sheriff Darter: Thanks for coming down to the station, Mr. Hall. Would you like something to drink?

Bill Hall: I'll take a Pepsi, Marcus, only if it's ice cold.

Sheriff Darter: I'm sure we can arrange that. We need to keep this formal, so please refer to me as Sheriff during the interview.

Bill Hall: Okay, Sheriff.

Sheriff Darter: Why were you in the woods yesterday morning?

Bill Hall: My beagle Lucy didn't come to the porch for supper the night before. I went out looking for her.

Sheriff Darter: Find your dog?

Bill Hall: No, Sheriff, I did not.

Sheriff Darter: That's a shame; Lucy is a good dog. You have anything with you that morning?

Bill Hall: Like what?

Sheriff Darter: Oh, like a walking stick, backpack, or maybe a dog leash?

Bill Hall: Naw, just what I got on right now, plus my hat.

Sheriff Darter: Deputy said you had a pair of gloves. Why did you have gloves?

Bill Hall: In case I found a dead dog.

Sheriff Darter: Why would you think you'd find your beagle dead?

Bill Hall: 'Cause I'd already found two of my dogs dead in the woods.

Sheriff Darter: Dead, how?

Bill Hall: Not sure; looked like they had been beat to death.

Sheriff Darter: Any idea who would have done that?

Bill Hall: Probably, damn kids.

Sheriff Darter: Did you know the victim?

Bill Hall: I would see Ms. Cardin at the ball field. I still raise the flag for the National Anthem, ya know? She was a teacher at the middle school.

Sheriff Darter: That's right. She was also once the Wheeler Diamond Queen.

Bill Hall: Oh, yeah, I remember her being that.

Sheriff Darter: A dead Diamond Queen remind you of anything?

Bill Hall: Those killings from years ago?

Sheriff Darter: You see anybody else that morning?

Bill Hall: No.

Sheriff Darter: How d'ya think she died? You touch her?"

Bill Hall: I dunno; her skin looked blue. Her eyes were bugged out. She have a heart attack?

Sheriff Darter: Murdered. She was strangled. You didn't answer my question. Did you touch her?"

Bill Hall: Naw, I didn't mess with the body. You don't think I had anything to do with that?

Sheriff Darter: We have to ask these questions.

Bill Hall: I'll help any way I can.

Sheriff Darter: Good. That's all I have for now, but don't roam too far. If you remember anything, let us know.

Bill Hall: Uh, Marcus, I mean Sheriff …

Sheriff Darter: What?

Bill: I never got my Pepsi.

6

Caleb sat at the last study computer in the back of the dimly lit library where they held evening detention. Tall shelves filled with ancient-looking books on outdated subjects flanked him on either side, while a dusty microfiche machine sat next to him in the corner. A lot of the school's equipment was a throwback to the eighties. This library made sense in a town that worshiped sports. The one thing that Caleb did like about the room was that it was quiet, except for the annoying hum of an overhead fluorescent rod that kept flickering on and off.

Caleb tapped his hand on the desk with one hand while squeezing a small lump of clay with the other. He was waiting for the outdated computer to boot up. He had trouble sitting still at the thought of playing on the baseball team. No one had ever asked him to play a sport, and his dream of being on the field during Homecoming, with everyone cheering, had always been one of his fantasies.

He looked around the empty library and noticed the only other kid there—a large boy with curly red hair wearing a skateboard shirt. Caleb had seen him before hanging out with Mark Mallory and Eric Frame. He was not a major Hyena, but he sometimes ran with the cackle. They locked eyes for a minute before each went back to what they were doing on their computers.

Caleb worked on his homework for a few minutes and then started looking through animal and monster videos on YouTube. After several videos, he stopped at a strange one entitled: *A Guide to Making Your own Tulpa.* Caleb thought it was an odd title, and this intrigued him enough to watch it.

"You two better not be surfing the internet for anything other than your schoolwork," the droll-sounding detention supervisor Mr. Jones snapped. "Better yet, I'll make a round in a minute to check your progress."

Caleb switched back to the screen with his homework assignment as the detention hall teacher walked by and leaned over his shoulder.

"Good, Mr. Jenkins. You are new to these hallowed halls of detention?"

"Y-yes, sir."

"Hopefully you'll use your time wisely, unlike most of the rabble that comes through here," he added, before walking back to the front of the room.

As soon as the man passed, Caleb switched back to the video and reached down to grab his headphones.

The girl in the video had blue hair, a soft voice, and bright eyes. *"Are you lonely and don't have a friend that you can count on?"*

Caleb perked up and nodded at the screen.

"What if I told you that you could create a friend - a best friend? First step is to train your brain to think for two people, not just one. You must learn to react to stimuli from the perspective of an imaginary personality other than your own. So, how do you train yourself to look and listen as someone else, but still remain you? You start by sculpting the image of this friend in your mind's eye and then talk to them. Can you close your eyes and picture the face of your Tulpa?"

"Y-yes," Caleb whispered.

"What does your future best friend look like? What color eyes does he or she have? What do their hair and nose look like?"

Caleb's skills as a sculptor came in handy with visualizing his imaginary friend. He could see his potential Tulpa's face as clearly as he saw the freckle-faced boy seated across from him.

The overhead light dimmed.

The easily annoyed Mr. Jones looked up at the light and shook his head.

Caleb glanced up to make sure he didn't get up. Satisfied, he dove back into the screen.

"Now, see the rest of their body and how they move. What does their smile look like? Make them walk around in your imagination. You can do anything you want with your Tulpa. You can go on fantastical adventures in your imagination with them, and—if you work hard enough on your creation—you may even see your Tulpa start to think for themselves."

Caleb nodded again. The idea of bringing a Tulpa to life, and never feeling alone, made him super happy. The image of the boy was already forming in his mind. He based it on himself a little, and what a brother would look like.

The girl showed a picture of her Tulpa. It was a cartoon unicorn, also with blue hair like its creator.

"My Tulpa's name is Sparkle Horn, and he is my bestie. Now, can you hear your Tulpa's voice? If you can't, then maybe start by asking him or her some questions."

There was silence for a good minute, but then he heard a distinct voice pop into his mind. It sounded like it was coming from a place far away, but it came out of Caleb's mouth.

"G-Gren," Caleb said.

"Quiet!" The detention teacher shouted.

Caleb hunkered down. *Beowulf* was his favorite book. The monster in the book was named Grendel. The story took place in the 6th century and was about a group of heroes coming to aid the ailing Hrothgar, King of the Danes. An outcast monster called Grendel was plaguing the King's great mead hall. Caleb had always felt like Grendel was the real victim. It was the bullies that hunted the monster and killed his mother.

"Okay, time's up! Start putting away your items, you are free to go," the detention teacher said.

Caleb stopped watching the video and removed his earphones. The animated host of the podcast kept talking but, unknown to Caleb, the subject grew darker as she laid out some dire warnings about creating a Tulpa for selfish reasons. The subtitles that flashed at the bottom of the screen were accompanied by skull and crossbones, like a label found on poison.

WARNING

'Tulpamancery must be approached with pure intentions and with maturity, anything less than this will have dire consequences. It is a sentient life-form you are creating. I recommend that you be at least over sixteen before trying this. A message to all thirteen- and fourteen-year-olds out there, and people around that age—you are not mature enough to manifest a Tulpa! This is not meant to be an insult, by no means, but you must be mentally secure enough to create another sentient life. I only mention this as a warning. If you create them for the wrong reasons—such as for revenge, or to replace a lost loved one—the Tulpa may have an identity crisis and grow angry. It could potentially hurt you and those around you. I can promise *you this."*

7

Caleb could see Mark Mallory and his pack of Hyenas were waiting for him just outside the school's front doors. The red-headed kid in detention must have told them he was there. He turned and started walking at a faster pace toward the gymnasium. His plan was to go through the back doors that led to the baseball field and take his usual path through the woods to his house.

The gym floor was nearly mirror-like, having been freshly polished. Caleb made his way to the double metal doors.

"Hey, get off the floor!" the volleyball coach yelled.

"S-sorry," Caleb said and started walking faster but slipped a little in the process.

The girls' volleyball team was just ending their practice, and Mark Mallory's girlfriend Lexi was among them. She spotted Caleb, grabbed her cell phone and started texting.

Caleb veered left and ran out the metal doors into the light, just as Mallory and his lieutenant Eric Frame were coming around the corner. Caleb took off in a dead sprint toward the ball field and the woods behind it.

"He's getting away!" Eric said.

The Hyenas caught up with Caleb just as he had leapt over the chain fence and dropped down into center field.

"Where you think you're going, Clay Tard! Mark yelled as he easily jumped the fence and tackled the out-of-breath boy to the ground. His backpack rolling across the green, his pants getting ripped and stained.

"Here, take my phone. I want a video of this," Eric said to Mark.

Eric was on top of him in seconds.

A smiling Mark held up the phone.

Caleb raised his hands, thrashing back and forth, in a vain attempt to block some of the blows.

"Move a little. I want to get his face on here, Mark said.

"Hey! What are you doing over there!" Sam Darter yelled from one of the dugouts.

A startled Eric stopped pummeling Caleb and stood up.

"Oh, shit … it's Coach," Mark said. "Let's go!"

Sam was walking toward the group.

Eric stomped Caleb's hand before leaving. "See ya later … weirdo!"

Caleb screamed with pain, as he rolled over.

Sam reached him and helped him up. "You okay, Caleb?"

"I … I'm okay," he said, favoring his hand. Blood and grass tatted his body and clothes.

"Wait right here," Sam said. He could see Mark and Eric walking fast around the side of the building.

Sam jumped the fence and headed in their direction.

He caught the two just before they disappeared around the corner. They were admiring their recent video and laughing, but as Sam approached, they switched it off.

Sam snatched the phone from Eric's hand.

"You think this is funny?"

"No, Coach," Mark said. "That kid started it. He's psycho."

"I see you messing with him one more time, and I will kick you off the team."

The two of them just stared.

"Let me know you understand."

"I understand," Eric said.

"Mallory?"

"Yeah, I understand."

"Good, now go over and apologize to Caleb," Sam said and pointed toward the field.

"But he's not there anymore."

Sam looked for Caleb, but he was nowhere to be seen.

"Can I go? My dad needs help washing the car," Eric said.

"Go," Sam said and turned to walk away.

"What about my phone?"

"I'm keeping it for a few days."

Mark waited until Coach Darter was out of sight. "We are gonna make Clay Boy pay for this."

"But Coach said …"

"I heard what he said, but I've got an idea. It's gonna be epic," Mark said.

8

Dr. Barry Dorjee was born in Tibet to a Tibetan father and an American mother. After his father's death when he was ten, Dorjee's mother had taken him back to the US, where he would study medicine, later specializing in the arcane and paranormal as well as the more traditional aspects of psychiatry.

His knowledge and specialties were vast. He had attained a PhD. in abnormal psychology at a young age and advanced degrees in philosophy, history, world religion, and even fringe parapsychology. He had written several books on fringe subjects including a study of the Tulpa and its correlation to the more innocent—and far less harmful—phenomenon of the childhood imaginary friend.

Dorjee worked in a mental health center in Los Angeles during his postgraduate studies at USC. The center treated patients with extreme psychosis and split personality disorder. Dorjee's unique background involving studies of parapsychology led him to help people both with traditional problems and with issues of the paranormal.

Although raised in Tennessee, he grew up to live his life by a set of rules known as the Five Precepts: a promise to abstain from killing any living being, stealing, sexual misconduct, lying, and intoxication.

Dorjee had met Caleb Jenkins just after he had started the ninth grade, and who was to become the main focus of his acclaimed, and sometimes derided, master work *Ancient Voices Within Us*. Caleb's Aunt Lois had contacted him after seeing an article he had written about children's imaginary friends which touched on the phenomenon of Tuplamancery.

As Lois outlined her nephew's tragic history and described his behavior, standing out in the rain, not remembering the past few hours, and other significant incidents, Dorjee knew that fourteen-year-old Caleb met all of the criteria.

Dorjee had watched as the woman and the boy approached his offices in the West Side Medical Center. He saw Caleb hesitate as they walked toward the large glass double doors of the ten-story grey building, craning his neck up at the immense glass structure.

As they walked into his consulting rooms, the doctor saw Caleb pull out a small lump of clay, holding tight to it as if he were holding his best friend's hand.

"Mrs. Jenkins, Caleb, welcome. Please come inside," Dorjee greeted them, with a warm and inviting smile. His rooms had a definite Eastern religious vibe. A large statue of a multi-armed deity spanned the far wall. Several paintings of yoga poses filled the rest of the room.

"I saw you on the TV and read your book," Lois said while staring in awe at the scary statue in the corner.

"You've caught me red-handed," the doctor replied with a southern drawl.

"I'm sorry I called so late last night."

"That's perfectly okay. Please make yourself comfortable, Mrs. Jenkins. You too, Caleb."

"Say hello, Caleb."

"H-hi," Caleb said, looking around with curiosity at all the exotic items in the room, which were a nerdy teen's dream come true. Action figures lined one side of the wall, and original comic book art too. It was an eclectic mixture of pop culture and Eastern religious statues.

The doctor waved his hand for Lois to sit down. She was careful not to walk too close to the glaring statue.

There were several collectible toys on a shelf. Caleb went over to them and touched one of the action figures' swords.

"You like Gundam?" the doctor said.

"What's a G-Gundam?" Caleb replied.

"You don't know Gundam? You look like you would be an anime fan. It's about giant robots with advanced human pilots. It is very cool stuff."

A sour-faced Lois shook her head. "We don't allow silly things like that into our home."

"I find giant robots therapeutic. Go ahead and pick it up. Can I get you some hot tea, Mrs. Jenkins?"

"I suppose," she said.

"Cool!" Caleb said, picking up one of the more colorful ones.

"No, I don't drink hot tea," she answered, still taking in the exotic room.

"People in the south tend to like sweet iced tea, and I do drink it on occasions, but I spent a great deal of time in London during my schooling. I know it's kinda funny that I still have this thick Southern accent. You might think I should be singing down on Music Row instead of being a therapeutic doctor. You really should try this new tea I picked last week. It's a jasmine, and so tasty."

"Oh, I guess when in Rome, or wherever this is," she said. She was starting to relax a little. "Just no sugar, please."

"Legend has it that in ancient Tibet, a king had a serious illness, and during his recovery, a beautiful bird he had never seen before flew into his window holding a branch with a few fragrant leaves on it. The king plucked the leaves from the branch and tasted them. They tasted good, and he thought that boiling them would make a good drink," the doctor said, stirring one of the cups and handing the tea to Lois. "And that's how tea came to Tibet, supposedly."

"Thank you. I've never heard that story."

"I read a lot, and I am fascinated with myths and legends."

Lois took a nervous sip. "Why do you have a statue of a demon in your office?"

"Oh, you mean the Dharmapala? She is no demon but a protector against hidden enemies. She helps people personify their better nature. There is a duality in people, two natures; one is a higher vibration while the other is lower. They should always be in balance, but in some cases, one overtakes the other. My job is to correct that imbalance. The balance between good and evil within a person's soul."

Lois was unsure how to respond to that because she knew that evil was ugly, and that statue looked as ugly as the Devil himself. "I'm sorry, but it looks like a demon."

"Demons are found within the Christian pantheon of supernatural beings. Actually, the word demon originated from the ancient Greek word daemon. It means a lesser deity, or spirit, not necessarily good or evil," he said between quick sips.

"I'm a Christian, and in Christianity, demons are evil. My husband is a prophet."

"Really?" he said. "I'm a bit of a holy man myself. I'm a Buddhist monk, albeit a little unorthodox, but I do adhere to the moral precepts set forth by the doctrine."

"A monk? You're a monk?" Lois said, putting her hands over her eyes.

"I know. I don't look like your typical monk. I'm not going to ask you to snatch a pebble from my hand or anything, but the precepts of my beliefs give me a clarity."

"The reason I brought Caleb here is because I saw you on the show talking about imaginary friends. He has one that he spends an abnormal amount of time with, and I think it's not healthy for a boy his age. I think it is the way he is dealing with the loss of his mother. He's always in the woods near our house, and I'm worried about him. He started mentioning the thing you were talking about in your book and on that show. You called a Talpa?"

"A Tulpa."

"Yes, that thing."

"You talked a little on the phone about the trauma in his past involving his mother, your sister?"

"My son came to live with us after my sister's death. I mean, technically he is my nephew, but I love him as my own son."

Barry's face grew more serious. "How did she die? What were the circumstances?"

Lois looked over at Caleb, who was exploring other items on the far side of the room. She lowered her voice before continuing.

"Her body was found beside the interstate. She was a victim of a serial killer," she said as she picked lint off her skirt and jacket and glanced again at her nephew. "Is that the reason he's acting out by creating this imaginary thing?"

"I am so sorry for your loss. Having a person create an imaginary friend to cope with trauma is not extraordinary, and it doesn't necessarily mean that his imaginary friend is a Tulpa. That is a different matter entirely. I hope we are not dealing with a Tulpa."

"How do we know? He is constantly whispering and laughing with this imaginary friend. And, I know you will probably think that I'm crazy, but I've seen things happen, and Caleb says he didn't do it," she said.

Caleb looked over at them. "H-hello? I'm standing right here. I'm n-not a little kid."

"My nephew seems to know things that he couldn't possibly know. My husband won't admit it, but I think he's scared of Caleb."

Dr. Dorjee sat back, took a sip of tea, and raised an eyebrow. "Is this true, Caleb? Do you think your uncle is afraid of you?"

"I don't know."

"If he is, why do you think he would be?"

"A teacher of his got her nose broken in class. Caleb was involved. We also woke up one night with Caleb standing over our bed."

"Caleb, why were you in their room?"

"I j-just woke up there."

"Did you hurt your teacher on purpose?"

"I didn't throw the clay."

"Who did then, your friend?"

I don't know if I believe in this Tulpa nonsense, but isn't it just another way to say that Caleb could have a personality disorder, right?"

"We don't call it that any more. It's called Dissociative Identity Disorder, but it's okay. I don't think it's that, and real Tulpas are rare, and this might not be the case, but we should investigate the possibility. I have only encountered one real case."

"What's going on, then?"

"That's what we are going to find out."

The toy robot slammed onto the floor and broke into pieces.

"Caleb?" Lois said. "Did you do that on purpose?"

He looked confused.

"It's okay," Dr. Dorjee said.

"Do you believe in the Devil, doctor?" Lois asked.

"I believe in the balance of good and evil, and sometimes that battle manifests in very different ways, but the shadow is in us."

"Can you help my nephew?"

"I would like to speak with him alone for a few minutes if that's okay?"

"Caleb, I'll be in the hallway. Thank you, Dr. Dorjee."

"Please, call me Barry."

"Okay, I'll be right outside. Mr. Dorjee" She looked back and smiled at Caleb as she stepped into the hall.

Caleb pulled a lump of clay from his pocket.

"So, Caleb, here we are," Dr. Dorjee said, staring intently at the boy and trying to get a read on his mood.

Caleb continued manipulating the clay.

"Why did you throw the robot down?"

He looked up wide-eyed at the doctor. "I-I didn't. It was an accident."

"But we just saw you do it."

"Gren gets angry when p-people say bad things about me."

"Are you just using Gren as a scapegoat for acting out? I get it, we all get angry at times."

Caleb looked away.

"What are you sculpting?"

"A b-bird."

"Can I take a closer look at it?"

Caleb got up from his cross-legged position, walked over to the doctor, and placed the bird in his hand. Barry was taken aback by the realness of the sculpture. He kept moving his fingers lightly over the feathers and beak. It was as if a 3D printer made it from an actual photo.

"This is amazing work, Caleb. It looks like it could flap its wings and fly around my office. Why do you sculpt birds?"

"I like them."

This is a sparrow, I believe?" Dr. Dorjee said. The teen's demeanor shook him a little, and his patients rarely made him nervous, except for one other. "Is that right? I used to be a bit of a bird-watcher, but I'm a little rusty these days."

"I s-see them in the w-woods," Caleb said.

"Do you ever have blackouts, Caleb?"

"I sometimes l-lose track of time and am late for d-dinner. You c-can have the b-bird. I'm sorry about the robot."

"I will put it on the shelf."

Caleb stared blankly.

The lamp blinked beside them and fell off the table.

The doctor dropped his tea.

"Is everything okay?" Lois asked, having stuck her head back into the room.

"He did fine. I will be in touch to schedule another appointment. Caleb, it was good meeting you."

Caleb nodded, as Lois placed her arm around him and they left.

Dorjee went to pour himself more tea, but stopped, when he heard what sounded like wings fluttering."

He looked around the office and settled on the shelf where he had out Caleb's bird. It was missing."

There was a rattling in the ceiling. It was the same fluttering of wings he had just heard.

He grabbed a chair and dragged it under the noise and climbed up on it to get closer to the source. It sounded like a bird was trapped behind the tiles.

Dorjee had to stretch in order for his fingertips to barely touch the ceiling panel. He pushed the foam panel up a few inches to get a better look at whatever was making the racket.

An old childhood fear of birds rushed back up to the surface, as he peered into the slit of darkness. There was definitely something alive in there, something that was flailing itself against the other boards over and over. He lengthened his body another inch just as the chair tipped over and caused him to fall hard.

Dorjee wasn't sure how long he had been knocked out. When he sat up, he noticed the clay bird was laying just a few feet from him near an overlooked piece of the broken robot. The only sound now was his heart pounding in his chest.

9

Sheriff Marcus Erwin Darter was a no-nonsense man with old-school sensibilities. He belonged in a Louis L'Amour novel, more than modern-day, with his cowboy hat and western boots. He had fought two tours in the Gulf War and worked at various odd jobs upon returning to civilian life.

Marcus became a deputy in the Frankfort Sheriff's Department in the late '90s, eventually becoming sheriff. That was no easy feat for a town that had never had a Black man in the position. Plus, it had been only a few months into Marcus's first year as active sheriff, in 2009, when they found the body of twenty-six-year-old Claire Conroy in the tall weeds off Highway 40.

Marcus spotted Sam, dressed in blue jeans and a Wheeler Wildcats ball cap, crossing the street from the post office. Sheriff Darter got out of his cruiser and walked over, feeling nervous about what he'd say to his son after all this time. He put on the warmest smile he could muster as he approached his son.

They locked eyes.

"Dad?" Sam said and started physically shaking, mostly from anger and the residual fear from his childhood.

"Sam. I figured we'd see one another eventually. You gettin' settled in?"

"Yeah."

"Marie and Helen here?"

"Look, I'm gonna be late getting to the ball field."

Marcus removed his cowboy hat and took a deep breath, trying to steady his large hands and deliver the next few words as smoothly as possible. "Son, I know things haven't been ideal between the two of us for a long time, but you've got to stop blaming me for everything."

"Mom was sick back then, and she needed you, but you were too busy with the ghosts of all those dead girls," Sam said with both fists clenched. "You were obsessed with it."

Marcus waved his hat back and forth, and his old anger bubbled to the surface. "You know your mother battled depression her entire life, and

I'm not saying that I don't carry some of the blame, but you've got no idea the pressure this town put on me to find the person responsible for those killings and when I didn't, they all blamed the Black sheriff."

"You know what I do know?"

"What's that?"

"How the back of my father's hand feels after a few drinks. And don't you dare start on how hard it is to be a Black man in this country-assed town. I know how hard it is. Mom needed you, but you'd rather curl up in the coffin with a bunch of dead girls."

Sam's fists relaxed. He had wanted to say these things for a long time.

The sheriff smiled. "You finished, got that all out of your system?"

Sam was still shaking.

"He's back."

"What are you talking about?"

"We found a body. One of your teachers. Killed just like Claire Conroy. We haven't talked to the press much, but it's bound to come out soon."

"Jesus, which teacher?"

"Art teacher, a Jessica Cardin. I think you went to high school with her."

"Yeah, she was a cheerleader. Pretty girl, from what I remember. She was the Diamond Queen back then."

"He has a type, always has."

"Why would he wait all this time just to come back now?"

"I wish I knew. We're waiting for forensics to verify if the prints match, but I feel it in my bones; it's the same damn guy. It's the Cove Strangler."

"God, here we go again," Sam said as he crumpled his coffee cup and tossed it in a nearby trash bin.

"I always loved you and your mother, and I would like a chance to show love to my only granddaughter if you just give me the chance."

Sam took a deep breath. "Don't give me that bullshit! Not now!" Sam pointed at his father. "Look, don't you fucking dare come anywhere near my family. It's my family, and you aren't bringing your poison to my doorstep. You left that responsibility a long time ago when you became obsessed with that sicko. Now, your drug is back."

"Aw, son, it may not be all up to you. That girl has a mind of her own, and sooner or later she's gonna want to meet her grandpa. This is a small town."

Sam walked right up to his father. His face locked in rage, an old rage.

"I'm not scared of you anymore, old man," Sam said. "Now, get out of my way before I knock your ass out." He pushed his father out of his way and continued across the street.

Marcus smiled and called after Sam, "Looks like you still got that Darter temper. Great running into you, son."

10

From *Ancient Voices Within Us All: A Study of Tulpamancery* by Doctor Barry Tenzin Dorjee, PhD, Pg. 27:

I have encountered a few instances of what I have termed Tulpamancery, but nothing like the case of my current thirteen-year-old male patient, Caleb Jenkins.

His mother, Claire Conroy, got pregnant with her son while running from the law. She had fallen in love with a small-time drug dealer named Royce Landau; she had been in the car the night that Royce ripped off a rival meth-head, and, in the process, killed him.

My notes in an earlier chapter mentioned that Royce Landau was eventually shot to death after a car chase with police on a hot summer night in Southern Mississippi. This is after he had abandoned the new mother Claire in Decatur, Alabama, a month earlier. This all took place in the summer of 2009.

After the incident, the mother attempted to hitchhike to her childhood home of Wheeler's Cove, Tennessee. It is believed that is where she unknowingly accepted a ride from the *Cove Strangler*. Her body was found by the side of Interstate 40, just a few miles from her hometown. Claire Conroy had been a former Wheeler Diamond Queen.

A deputy, Marcus Darter, had just been appointed to the position of sheriff, and upon arriving at the scene found the strangled body of the girl, and an eleven-month-old baby, whom I now know to be Caleb, was wrapped in her jacket and placed in tall grass, as if someone didn't want him to get hurt, and if it hadn't been for the protection of his mother's jacket, he would have most certainly died from exposure.

At approximately 10 a.m. Nov. 1st, the following day, Lois Jenkins, her married name, younger sister of Claire Conroy was informed that her sister's body had been found, and that her sister's one-year-old son, Caleb, was being held by child protective services. Lois and her husband Nestor were allowed to take the child home that very day, later adopting the boy and raising him as their own.

Early on, when Caleb was three, his aunt told me that she would frequently find him playing and having conversations with an imaginary friend. These exchanges only lasted until Caleb was four, but that's when the bad dreams started. He would wake up screaming at all hours of the night. The death and destruction in the small community of Wheeler's Cove, Tennessee could have been prevented, if people had understood what they were dealing with. This phenomenon is real; it has destroyed many lives and left another of my patients to live the remainder of her life in a psychiatric facility. Through the course of this study, I will try and show what happened to my patient and the phenomenon was created and turned violent.

11

Caleb's hand was still throbbing from Eric Frame stomping on it. He always liked cutting through the small patch of woods between Wheeler Middle and his house. This woodlot was his favorite place in the world, where he would spend countless hours building forts and reading books. He often sat by the small stream that curved like a snake through the pine grove. He loved how the clean water sparkled like tossed diamonds over a sheet of sunshine and how quiet it was here. These woods were a holy place to him and better than his uncle's church.

He took off his shoes to put his bare feet in the icy water and then grabbed a handful of red clay from the thick bank. His hand was starting to feel better, so he began sculpting tiny butterflies and dragons, but the instructions from the Tulpa video still echoed in his mind. He closed his eyes to picture the boy again and found the image was still strong in his mind's eye.

"I h-hate those idiots!" he said. "I wish they were d-dead."

He felt pressure in his head. A wild breeze whipped across the top of the water and over him. There was an odd feeling that another presence was nearby.

"You d-don't have to be shy. I know what it's l-like to be scared all the t-time."

Caleb dug up a lump of raw clay and started sculpting it into a boy. He worked quickly, reaching to pick up a stick so he could detail the finer features of his cheeks and expression.

"I made you in clay, see?" Caleb said and held up the creation. "This is the way I see you in my m-mind," he said, closing his eyes and visualizing his imaginary friend.

An errant and chill breeze whipped across Caleb moving his hair to the side.

"Gr … en," a voice said, sounding like it came from some faraway place.

Caleb's eyes opened. "Whoa, w-where are you?"

"In da-ark."

"C-can you come into the light?"

The sinking sun shot needles of light through the branches of the trees and across the water. Caleb noticed it and jumped to his feet. "Oh no, I-I am going to be late for dinner. I have to g-go." He pulled on his shoes and sat the small statue of Gren on the ground.

"Fr-fr-friend stay."

"I promise I'll come back tomorrow, but I can't be late for dinner," the boy called as he ran down the path toward home.

Caleb thought Gren lived in the woods, but he was wherever Caleb was. The Tulpa needed to protect him. He had been buried in the darkness since Caleb's mother had been murdered, but Gren didn't want to stay in the darkness anymore.

12

Helen Darter walked through the bright aisles of the Wheeler's Cove Video Store, checking out the rows and rows of DVDs and Blu-Rays, then stopped in front of a large VHS section. "Where the hell am I?" she said to herself, a look of awe on her face. "This is awesome."

She took a VHS box down and looked at it like a lost relic from some ancient time. Helen could have created this entire section. It had nearly every movie she loved and many she couldn't find anywhere.

Her father had big plans for her to attend an Ivy League college to become a doctor or lawyer, but the thing she loved most were movies, especially horror and monster movies.

She spied a lanky, red-haired clerk watching her from behind the counter. He looked around her age and wore all black like her, but she hadn't seen him at school. He pretended to listen to a customer chattering away about some terrible movie, but she saw that he was checking her out.

"Welcome to Video Store!" he shouted. He'd been staring at Helen since she walked through the front door.

The older lady that he was talking to looked peeved, as the clerk left her and focused his attention on Helen.

"This place is amazing, but the name could use some work."

The boy made his way over to greet her while he fiddled with his shaggy hair and tried to stand taller than his five foot eight. "I would have named it *The* Video Store, but alas, I am just a lowly clerk. You like late eighties and early nineties horror movies? If so, I'm responsible for this section, and if not—I don't know who the hell did that."

He rubbed his tousled head and looked a little like a lost puppy. She tried to hide that she found him pretty cute by not smiling too much.

"I love them, and this is a rad VHS section," she said, running her fingertips across the old boxes. "I've always felt like I should've been born in the late eighties, early nineties, but I'm stuck in the decade of pandemics and bland corporate music."

"I want to say we did it to be all retro-cool, but the Corny Cove is stuck in a time warp. I mean, we don't even have a Starbucks, for Christ's sake."

"The *Corny* Cove?" she asked with a sideways glance.

"That's what people trapped here call it, and the fact that everywhere you look, you see cornfields. Hi, my name is Donny Mayer, but my friends call me Scares."

"Scares?" Helen said. "You don't look too scary with your lovely strawberry locks."

"Yeah, because of my passion for horror movies." He reached out for a fist bump, which she awkwardly returned.

"Fist bump?"

He jerked back his hand and coughed. "I am a bit of an expert in eighties and nineties horror and also blessed with good hair."

"Helen Darter, fugitive of boredom and seeker of the darkness."

"Nice life mission you got there. Are you a bored vampire that can just happen to walk in the daylight?" he asked, trying to puff his chest out and lower his voice to impress her.

"Maybe?" she said and bared her teeth. "You gotta live your life to the fullest, man. Who knows, you may end up at summer camp having lots of unsafe sex one minute and then get stabbed by a madman in a hockey mask the next," she said, brushing her hair behind her ear.

"Ah, you like the quality classic horror films!"

"Oh wow, you have *April Fool's Day*?" she said, bringing down the box to read the back.

"That movie was one of three horror films from 1986 that take place on April Fool's Day, the others being what?"

Helen scoffed. "Come on, really? The others are *Killer Party* and *Slaughter High*."

"Oh, wow—I'm impressed. I prefer *My Bloody Valentine*. Who's your favorite director?"

"The G.O.A.T … John Carpenter."

"Good choice! I also do special effects for horror movies."

"Oh, yeah? What have you done?"

"Well, I plan on doing special effects for *my* horror movie. I did the special effects for last year's school play at Wheeler Middle, but I'm working on my own independent feature film. It's gonna be called *Class Reunion at Hell Lake*. It's about a guy who invites his boyhood bullies to a reunion at an abandoned summer camp under the guise it's a class reunion, but in actuality, it's a trap, and he takes them out one by one with an ax, or a chainsaw, I haven't really decided yet."

"Oh, kinda like I Spit on your Grave mixed with Friday the Thirteenth?"

"Yes! You do understand my passion." Scares placed his hand over his heart and sighed.

"That has the potential to happen. I go to Wheeler Middle. You?"

"I do, I mean, did. I'm supposed to be in the ninth grade, but I'm kinda suspended for the rest of this year, and I've had other issues with the modern school system."

"What did you do to *kinda* get suspended?"

"I put a smoke bomb in the locker room, but they thought it was a real bomb and called in the bomb squad from Nashville. When they figured out that it was just a super smoke bomb, they just suspended me for the rest of the year. It could have been worse."

"Oh, wow. My dad would *love* you?"

"Really?"

"No."

"When did you move here?" He awkwardly changed the subject.

"Literally, three days ago, but my dad has been here for months."

"Might I ask why?"

"I lost a bet with fate," she said and shrugged her shoulders.

"Really? Big yikes."

"Actually, my family and me are in Witness Protection. We were in a cult, and things went south."

"No way! That is the coolest thing I've ever heard," Scares said.

"It's good that I can mold your mind to my will. I was kidding. My dad is the new principal and baseball coach at Wheeler Middle."

"Oh, that's why you said he might not like me. He's got his work cut out for him. The team sucks."

"I love your optimism."

"Yeah, living here pretty much sucks too."

"Why does it suck?" Helen asked and crossed her arms.

"It's full of meat-head jocks and dumbasses."

"I noticed. You ever heard of an idiot named Mark Mallory?"

"Oh yeah, he's both a bragging jock and a dumbass."

"He's in my art class."

"Sorry about that. Hey, like I said, me and my friends are going to shoot a horror movie this summer. You could be the main pretty girl who gets killed."

"I think of myself more as the killer," she said, miming the knife in the shower scene from Alfred Hitchcock's *Psycho*.

"I like you. Let me show you around the store," Scares said, moving closer and reaching over Helen's shoulder to pull down one of the empty movie boxes.

"That wasn't creepy," Helen said, raising her eyebrows.

Scare's face turned red.

"I'm just kidding, Casanova. It was pretty smooth in an awkward nineties *coming of age* movie kind of way."

"Take a look at this one. It's from the early nineties, but a damn good flick. A little more psychological horror than stab all in sight."

"*In the Mouth of Madness*? I can relate to that," she said as she moved a little closer to him. She had always been attracted to nerdier outsider types and Scares checked all of those boxes.

"We have OG black and white classics too, if you're into that. We have *Horror Hotel* and *Black Cat*."

"I haven't seen those."

"So, I do know some things about horror that you do not. Has anyone show you the Wheeler Cove sights?" he asked.

"You mean the Walmart parking lot?"

They both burst into laughter.

"We have all sorts of parking lots," he said. "Oh, and we have a lake and a Piggly Wiggly."

"What the hell is a *Piggly Wiggly*?"

"Just the finest grocery chain in the south. Come over to the counter, and I'll get the movie for you."

"Wait, my VCR broke on the move."

"You are welcome to watch them here. I mean after I close up. Some of us like to hang out here at night and eat candy, watch movies, and make plans for our movie. We call it *Friday Night Massacre*. We started doing it after the local theater closed down a few months ago."

"I've got to be somewhere tonight. My dad needs help at the ball field."

"Oh, that's okay," he said, as his shoulders slumped. "You wanna go for a ride in my van and listen to music? I'll give you the grand tour of Wheeler's Cove."

"Uh, your van?"

"Oh, I think I have an old VCR in the back you can borrow too if you want it."

"Awesome."

Scares ducked behind a dirty curtain into a small back room and reappeared with a VCR. "Here ya go. It should still work."

"Rad!" Helen picked up the movie and the VCR.

"Okay, just wait outside for me while I close up. It will only take a few minutes."

"But, your customer looks a little pissed," Helen nodded at a grumpy older lady staring a hole in them.

"Oh, Mrs. Brown, I forget you were there," Scares said in a syrupy Southern accent.

"I know you did."

Scares theatrically fainted into a row of movies, knocking the boxes onto the floor. He jumped up as if someone had shot electricity through his skinny frame and then leaped onto the sales counter with both hands held high above his head. "I suddenly don't feel well! I'm sorry, but I have to close the store early!"

Helen was in hysterics.

All of this was to the chagrin of a little old lady holding up a copy of *Fried Green Tomatoes*. "Excuse me," she said, "I'd like help finding all of Kathy Bates movies. Like I told you before I was rudely ignored. I have a local movie club I'm forming, and we're planning to watch all of Kathy Bates's movies."

"Pardon my behavior, ma'am, but I'm feeling faint. I think I may be coming down with something, so I must close up for the day. Pardon me for any inconvenience."

The lady gave him a hard look. Her glaring eyes peeking over the rim of her glasses. "You kids think old people are stupid? I know you just want to get off early to hang out with that girl. I'll go after you find me the movies on this list. Got it?"

"Okay, I'll find your Kathy Bates movies, calm down."

"I'll be waiting outside," Helen said, still laughing.

13

Deputy Dwight Greer had just gotten off work. He was still reeling from the excitement of the past few days. After the Sheriff had interviewed Bill Hall, he brought Dwight into his office and dropped a bombshell on him—the victim most likely had been killed by the Cove Strangler. Dwight nearly dropped his doughnut and coffee over this revelation. It was a big goddamned deal that one of the most notorious serial killers in modern times was back.

He tried to tell the Sheriff that he thought that Bill Hall was hiding something, but his boss seemed too busy or didn't believe the young Deputy, to really hear him. It seemed that no one really ever 'heard' him.

Dwight was still in his interceptor, which he usually drove home to his trailer in Drecherd every night. He loved to turn up the volume on his AC/DC tracks while blaring the sirens on the empty back roads. He was headbanging along when it suddenly dawned on him, as he drove past the Middle School and the ball field, that maybe he could find what Hall had stashed.

He stopped the car and looked over to the small patch of woods where the body had been found. This was his big chance to prove himself, he thought. He could even be the next sheriff of Frankfort County one day.

Dwight got out of the car. The sun was pretty low in the sky as he pulled up his utility belt and took a deep breath.

14

Helen was propped up on Donny 'Scares' Mayer's beat-up van when she saw the old lady exit the front door of the video store, and shortly after, Scares popped out. He turned and locked the door and shook it a few times. He was her type, the kid at school who wore all black and listened to heavy metal. She hadn't had a boyfriend in a while, but things were looking up.

"How did you know this was my van?"

"Just a lucky guess." She laughed, and slapped her hand on the painted grim reaper that adorned its side.

"I call her *The Destroyer!*"

"Maybe *The Destroyed* would be a better name?" she said and tilted her head.

"All that just gives her character," he said as they looked at the van.

The windshield had a crack down the passenger side; the paint job was a flat black, and the winged shadow demon on its side was amateurish.

Scares opened the door for Helen. "Your chariot, my lady!"

"I think you put the *corny* in Corny Cove with that one."

"Can't help it that I'm a *bona fide* gentleman," he said, slamming the door and running over and getting into the driver's side.

"So, where you taking me in your dark and scary van?"

"Me and the Destroyer are gonna give you the grand tour of the Cove."

"That sounds ominous and maybe fun?"

"Off we go!"

Scares started her up and they took off out of the parking lot.

"First stop, the Sonar Drive-In for a lime slushy, then we'll go to *Jump Off*."

She frowned. "What's *Jump Off*?"

"It's a bridge that people jump off of here … for fun."

"You locals really are that bored, huh?"

"It's a pretty good rush."

Helen thought the Tennessee countryside was beautiful, much different from the dry desert-like Los Angeles where the palm trees had been shipped in and planted with stolen mountain water. Everything back there was fake, a mirage, but there was nothing but green vegetation here.

She stuck her head out of the van window and took a deep breath. It smelled like damp grass to her, with a touch of sweetness, and she loved it. For the first time in a long time, she could breathe.

15

Excerpt from the online magazine Our Bizarre World, "Letting the Genie out of its Bottle" by Doctor Barry Tenzin Dorjee, PhD

Tulpas are matter developed by thought, crystallized mental energy. In Tibetan Buddhist and tantric beliefs as well, matter is created by thought. The Christian Bible, and most of the Western religions, say that God thought the universe into existence. What is that primal essence of creation? A force that is always near but cannot always be perceived. The Dhammapada says: "What we are today manifests from our thoughts of yesterday, and our present thoughts build our life tomorrow; our mind comes first before all physical matter. How is that so different from quantum physics? At some point, science and what we refer to as magic, must converge."

Tulpas are a supernatural phenomenon that are starting to be studied by Western researchers. The mind is not the new frontier—it is the only frontier.

There are many kinds of these manifestations, and they can take many incarnations. A Tulpa usually takes many months, even years, to create, though some have been known to accomplish the job much faster, usually those born with psychic abilities.

Tulpas acquire their own identity not long after they have completely formed. It is at that time they can become deadly; Tulpas vary in strength and power. It is like you have let a powerful genie out of its bottle. They can travel great distances from their creators and exhibit evil intentions. The worst of these having been born from tragedy or feelings of revenge. They have even been known to survive the death of their makers.

If the creator of the Tulpa dies, the creation will usually die with them, but it has been told that if its maker does not unmake the manifestation before death, it will continue on its own, roaming the world out of control, hurting or even possessing people. It has been highly debated on what to do if a person encounters one of these masterless Tulpas. Ancient texts have recommended finding a master yogi who can banish one as easily as they could create one. Paranormal experts, enlightened ones, tantrics, and some monks, those with evolved souls, also have the power to destroy these aberrations of thought.

16

Caleb loved to run, and he ran as fast as his legs could carry him toward home. The breeze on his face made him feel free, and he knew if he were late again for the prayer before dinner, his uncle would punish him. The fastest way home was to cut through Bill Hall's property, but the old farmer had trained a giant billy goat to attack anyone that crossed the fence onto his five acres.

The boy was a little hesitant to cross due to Ole Gruff. This demon goat was worse than any junkyard dog, and the angry creature had it in for Caleb. The last time the boy had dared to venture into the field, he had a close encounter with Ole Gruff that nearly got him pulled down and stomped. This goat was no ordinary farm animal, but Satan incarnate. His fur was black, with a ghost-white face and an impressive rack of curled horns that the old farmer had sharpened, or at least that was the rumor. The tale even went so far as to say a kid had died a few years back, and he was currently buried under some of the rusted farm equipment that littered the field.

Caleb scanned the entire field for any signs of the dreaded goat before he mounted the fence and dropped down to the other side. He started at a steady trot, all the while constantly keeping alert to any movement from his peripheral. After what seemed like an eternity, he finally reached the thickest part of the maze of rusted farm machinery. That's when he heard a loud grunt.

Caleb froze as he tried to decipher if the noise came from behind or ahead of him. He waited for a few seconds before starting to walk again, and just as he exited the gauntlet of immobile grain combines and cotton pickers, he saw Ole Gruff waiting for him.

"Baaah!"

Caleb sprinted toward the nearby fence.

Ole Gruff was just a few feet behind him with its head lowered.

The fence came up fast, and Caleb decided he would try and jump as high as he could to clear most of it and then flip head over heels to safety on the other side. It was risky, but anything was better than being gored by the goat.

Caleb leaped like a scalded cat onto the fence, and he had nearly made it to the other side when he felt the pinch of the goat's sharp teeth. It jerked the gasping boy backward. Both parties struggled back and forth, but the goat had started to win the tug of war. Caleb thought about the story of the boy from years ago being gored by the monster goat and supposedly buried under the old farm machinery. This gave him the extra jolt of energy he needed.

The terrified boy reached into his backpack and pulled out the baseball glove Coach Darter had given him, and in one swift movement, he slapped the goat across the face with the glove, causing ole Gruff to release him.

Caleb fell hard on the other side, but his shoe and glove stayed with the goat. He jumped up and backed away from the killer as it pawed the ground and let out a grunt of discontent over his young prey getting away. Caleb's mind was racing, and he couldn't believe he had survived the encounter.

The boy limped away toward the white two-story farmhouse in the distance. A stern-looking aunt Lois was there to greet him. She wore no makeup, but under her weathered exterior was a sweetness, an emotion she only displayed to a select few. It had been buried deep inside her years ago.

"What happened to your clothes? Did you get into another fight?"

"M-Mr. Hall's goat tried to get me," he said, keeping the fight a secret.

"I thought I told you not to go into that field, and where is your shoe?"

Caleb pointed back at the field and the goat.

"Get inside and eat your dinner. You missed the dinner prayer."

The inside of the old farmhouse hadn't changed much since Lois inherited it from her parents. It was a two-story simple design that had stood since the Civil War, and even though the outside paint had begun to chip, it had stood the test of time and, over the years, survived the countless tornadoes which plagued the area.

"Yes, ma'am."

Caleb walked past his scowling uncle Nestor. He was a slender man with a shiny complexion, as if he had tried to physically scrub away his sin, and he always dressed like he was on his way to church. He was a self-proclaimed prophet who often said that God spoke through him.

"Where you been?"

"I was walking b-back from school and c-cut through ole Bill Hall's field. His g—"

"No, I meant why did you have to stay after school?"

"I got d-detention."

"You broke a teacher's nose?" Uncle Nestor said and grabbed Caleb by the shoulder like he had done many times in the past. "I know that you and your aunt are tainted by something evil, but I promise you I'm gonna get that outta you."

Caleb hated to be touched. He tried to shrug off the grip but couldn't.

"You need to pray! And you will not be playing baseball! Your aunt told me the new coach called."

Caleb looked down as tears rolled down his cheeks, but the heat was also in his belly again. It was the same feeling he had while in art class with the bullies. The pressure in his skull was growing more and more intense.

"Look at me when I'm talking to you," Nestor said.

Caleb's eyes were hot from the tears and the heat that had moved from deep inside his guts to his throbbing head.

"Don't yell at me!" Caleb said, without a trace of a stutter and in a deeper, more menacing, voice. Caleb had gone away to somewhere dark. Gren was now in control.

Nestor leaned back. "I always knew you had a demon in you!"

Caleb latched on to the back of his uncle's head and, with his free hand, took a handful of mashed potatoes and shoved them into the gaping mouth of a stunned Nestor.

"Whaauhh?" Nestor tried to move away, but the boy had a powerful grip on his hair.

Caleb grabbed another handful of potatoes and stuffed them in his uncle's mouth. Nestor had now started to suffocate.

"Muhhhrupp!"

Stop!" screamed Lois, who had been watching from the doorway.

Caleb returned and was confused about his sudden outburst. He wasn't sure where it had come from.

Nestor was coughing as buttery potatoes dripped down his face and onto his shirt. He was in absolute shock as to what had just happened and didn't move.

"Does anyone need more iced tea?" Lois asked in hopes of breaking the tension.

Caleb looked down at his plate. "N-no, ma'am."

"Nestor?"

"Uh?" He looked at Caleb like he was the Antichrist. "Yes, please."

Caleb's fear turned to reveling in his new found power. "Did anyone say the prayer?" he said. "Okay, then I will. Father, please bless this meal that lays before us and watch over this family in good times and bad—amen."

17

It was a rainy Sunday morning, and salvation seekers filled the barn behind the Jenkins farmhouse to the brim. Caleb's aunt and uncle had converted her father's old barn into a makeshift church to start his *Church of the Miraculous Intent.*

Caleb sat beside his enthralled aunt Lois. He stared at the large stained glass behind his Uncle Nestor, who was on stage giving one of his fire-and-brimstone sermons that people seemed to lap up like stray cats drinking milk. It was flooding outside, and a steady stream of water poured down the stained-glass windows giving the illusion that Jesus wept over a praying shepherd and his flock of sheep below.

A clap of thunder made the sleepy young man snap out of his trance, and he locked eyes with his uncle. Nestor Jenkins was a corny mix of flashy showman and Dust Bowl-era mystic. He was ten years Lois's senior and she looked out of place by his side. He gave his growing and rabidly devoted congregation a show that was part blood on the cross salvation and part stage spectacular. Still, fear of retribution always drew people like moths to a flame, and Caleb could see his uncle light up from the attention he received.

"Mathew 24:32 says that we can learn a lesson from the fig tree. When its branches bud and its leaves begin to sprout, you know that the summer is near. The leaves of the fig are sprouting. We have famine, pestilence, nations against nations, extreme weather, and lawlessness. These are all signs of God's imminent return," he boomed out over the onlookers and flipped his heavy bible over to wave its cover like the wings of a living creature. He also stomped his foot on the wooden stage, which sounded like a hollow drum inside the room.

The church barn was packed, but you could hear a needle drop as people hung onto every word that fell out of the red-faced Nestor's mouth.

"History has shown us signs that the end is near, but now we are seeing all the signs coming to be. In Luke 21:28, Jesus said that when you see all of these things begin to happen, look up because your salvation is near.

God is showing us these things to let us know that we are in the last days. Last night, I had another vision."

The crowd gasped, and some shouted a loud, "Amen!"

Nestor walked across the stage to make sure no one in the congregation missed him but kept eyeing Caleb, who was still amazed at the fear in his uncle's eyes. Gren had promised that he would not have to be afraid of anyone, and his best friend was making good on that promise.

"I woke from my sketch pad. And as you all know, that's how the Lord bestows his gift of prophecy upon me from a bolt of lighting from the sky! I went to Heaven, but the Lord said I wasn't done here on Earth. He bestowed upon me these visions that I draw upon this pad. After receiving my last vision, I was completely horrified at what I had drawn. I saw a demonic black funnel tearing its way through the baseball field during the Homecoming Game. And I'd be amiss to not say that many people were lying dead."

There was a visible shudder from the crowd.

"My boy plays on the team!" came a worried voice from the congregation.

Caleb saw a woman pull her son tight to her side.

"The worst tornado in the history of the state is going to hit Wheeler's Cove in two weeks. I saw most of you at the baseball field in my vision. God is angry with us, whether you like it or not! Please pray with me, and please share the podcast of this sermon on all of your social medias when it is posted. Hopefully, the leaders of this town and community will take my gift seriously this time. Now, please lower your heads in prayer as we pass around our collection plate."

He shut his bible, held it to the sky, and started to speak in tongues. It was a sound that would make a random onlooker laugh, but to the initiated, it was the language of the divine.

Caleb always studied everyone when they had their heads down in prayer. He thought it was funny that some people only acted like they were putting money in the offering plate but would actually wad the bill deep into their palms to place it back into their pockets.

He also knew a secret about his uncle's gift of prophecy: it was a lie. God or the Devil hadn't given Nestor the gift of prophecy—it was given to his Aunt Lois.

18

From *Ancient Voices Within Us All: A Study of Tulpamancery* by Doctor Barry Tenzin Dorjee, page 40:

Lois Jenkins was also gifted psychically. She had the ability to see the future, and she passed this down to her nephew, but their gifts (or curse) were manifested slightly different. She would also go into a trance, but while in this state, she would sketch events that came true. There have been famous cases of psychic phenomena. Why they haven't been openly discussed as another form of unknown science until now is amazing to me.

There is much more to our realities than we care to admit, and we are only barely scratching the surface of what humans are capable of. I have seen enough in my career to make me steer my studies in the direction of what most term the paranormal. There are countless theories on how the brain functions and most scientists create experiments to glean the data that suits their theory. If they encounter data that doesn't fit their theory, they just ignore it.

A recent study showed seven out of nine non-psychics had variations in the intron (non-coding) region of their DNA, adjacent to a gene on Chromosome 7. By contrast, none of the psychic participants had that mutation.

Perhaps psychic powers were a natural thing for most of our ancestors, but for fear of being labeled evil or outcasts by society, people evolved to suppress the neural connections in the mind. I believe that evolution suppressed these traits. In mankind's recent past, we all depended on our intuition to gather food, avoid predators, and guess weather. Now, we have frozen dinners and fast food.

This perceptual ability is a muscle we no longer flex. The churches and the bible constantly speak of saints with supernatural powers but at the same time attempt to condemn and label these powers evil in others. After several visits with Caleb Jenkins, and his aunt, they were convinced to allow me to run tests on their DNA, but neither possess this mutation, but both their psychic abilities were suppressed. I feel like the 'norms' (non-psychic) make sense of the difference within people like Caleb and his aunt.

The most likely theorem is that everyone has some latent psychic abilities, and that they are passed down from one's ancestors, but we have yet to locate a biological marker that would inform an environmental or pharmacological way to enhance or to suppress the ability. Most likely it is true, that we are all born with paranormal potentiality, and one day we will discover that this is not paranormal, but very much normal.

19

The Conroy House

1999

"Loisy? Loisy! Please wake up," Claire said as she tried to wake her sister from one of her trances. Lois, at nine years old, looked like a small doll. Her hair was straight and hung long past the middle of her back. She was kneeling in the corner, scribbling furiously on the wall with a red crayon.

"Loisy!"

Lois suddenly came out of her trance with a confused look on her face.

"I had a dream that you were killed by a bad man, but you were not the way you look now; you were older," she said. Her innocent eyes were filled with tears.

"I'm not going to die. I'm right here now, silly," her fifteen-year-old sister said, trying to comfort her by running her fingers softly through her long hair.

"Sing to me, sissy," Lois pleaded. Music was the only thing that comforted her after one of her dreams.

"Okay, but you have to promise me that you will try to go back to sleep.

Lois nodded her head as Claire started to sing her favorite song.

"Oh, oh, oh, oh.
I'll always be there when you wake, yeah, yeah.
You know I'd like to keep my cheeks dry to-d-aay."

"I don't want you to die!" Lois blurted out as she fell into her sister's arms and held on like a person drowning.

"It's alright. It was just a bad dream," Claire told her little sister as she wiped away her tears and held her tight. "I'm always going to take care of you."

Innocent and scared eyes looked up at her. "What if you aren't here? Who will take care of me then?"

Claire smiled, wiping away her tears. "Let's close our eyes and imagine a protector to take care of you when I'm not here."

Lois closed her eyes.

"You got them closed?"

"Lois nodded her head."

"Now, imagine someone."

"Like God?"

"Does that make you feel safe?"

She nodded.

"Then that's fine."

"I love you."

"Look at me, Loisy. I'm not gonna let Daddy or anyone else call you bad. You are a special person."

"You are special too."

They hugged.

The intricate drawing on the wall showed a shadowy figure strangling an older Claire from behind. Lying in the tall grass beside her was a screaming baby. It wasn't the first dream Lois had had, but it was the most terrifying. All of her previous dreams had come true. She tried to close her eyes and go to sleep, but she feared she'd return to the field and the vision.

20

The creek that Caleb often played by had risen a little since Dwight had been there to inspect the crime scene just a few days ago. It was still roped off with the yellow tape, but the tape had sagged a bit, probably disturbed by a deer, or by local kids, running through it.

The deputy bent down, picked up a handful of the thick red clay that lined the bank and squeezed it in his hands until it oozed out through his thick fingers. He remembered seeing Bill Hall tuck a pair of gloves in his pocket and tossing something into a lump of weeds and rotten wood, just a few feet away.

Dwight tossed the clay to the ground and walked over to the wood debris. He crouched down and stuck his hand deep inside the rot and damp foliage, feeling around for something—anything—and then his fingertips ran over something that felt like a cable.

"Bingo!"

He grabbed it and pulled his hand back. He held what appeared to be an electrical cord.

"I got you, fucker!"

A twig snapped behind him.

"Who's there?" he said, his voice quivering a bit. He placed his hand on the top of his service revolver and spun around, drawing his weapon.

"Gotcha!"

He scanned the length of the creek and surrounding trees, as far as his eyes would go, but there was no-one there.

Dwight sighed, laughing at himself for being so spooked.

"I need to calm down."

He placed his gun back into its holster and tightened the muddy cord in his hands.

"The Sheriff is gonna promote the hell out of me for this."

A flock of black birds scattered on the other side of the creek as the sun ducked behind the clouds and the area darkened.

The space around him became dead quiet.

Someone stepped out from behind the tree on the other side of the bank. The sun was at their back, so they appeared in silhouette.

"You scared the shit out of me!" he said and shook his head in disgust. "What are you doing out here creeping around?"

The shadowy figure remained silent.

Dwight squinted his eyes. "Are you gonna say anything?"

The sun ducked behind a cloud, and the woods became even darker.

21

There were bright blue skies over Caleb's head this Monday morning as he walked down the same deer trail he took through the woods every day to get to school. He tossed a baseball high in the air and tried to catch it, but it was a lot harder without his glove. He knew he had to go back into the field to retrieve it before practice, but he didn't want to tangle with Ole Gruff again. He had barely escaped with his life last time.

A bird high up in a tree abruptly stopped singing, and Caleb felt another presence close to him. It frightened the boy at first, but then he closed his eyes and envisioned the image of Gren. "G-Gren?"

Silence.

The wind kicked up through the trees, and Caleb felt the pressure in his head. It wasn't quite a headache but was progressively getting worse every time he had an encounter with his Tulpa.

"So, I-I am going to be on the baseball team. Do you like b-baseball?" A noise from above in the trees made Caleb stop. "H-hello? G-Gren?" Something slapped the ball out of his hand.

He turned to find Mark Mallory and Eric Frame beside him. They had been waiting behind a tree for Caleb to walk past. He thought about running, but he knew it was futile.

"Hello, Clay Bitch!" Eric Frame said with the look of a smiling jackal. He stood beside the king of the Hyenas—Mark Mallory.

"Why are you standing out here talking to yourself?" Mallory asked.

"He's nuts. He saw his mommy get choked to death right in front of him," Eric Frame said, and acted like an invisible killer was choking him.

"No one to save your crazy ass now," Mark said as he held an old piece of a water hose. "What were you doing out here? Are you high or just retarded?" He backed Caleb against a tree, all the while slapping the hose against his leg.

"The little baby looks like he's gonna piss himself," Eric said.

Caleb saw a terrible thought forming in Mark's eyes.

"Let's hang him from one of those branches."

Caleb tried to fight them off and run, but Eric grabbed him, locking him into a full nelson.

"This is gonna hurt me a lot more than it hurts you." Mark laughed, then slapped Caleb across the face with the hose before looping it around the boy's neck.

Caleb had a terrible fear of not being able to breathe. He closed his eyes and concentrated on conjuring the image of Gren in his mind's eye.

Eric found a long vine and interlaced it through the tied hose, tossing the vine over a low-hanging limb.

"Okay. Let's pull him up," Mark said.

Eric hesitated. "I thought we were just gonna scare him a little, not actually hurt him?"

"What do you think we're doing?" A wild-eyed Mark said. "What, you're not pussin' out on me, are you?"

"Naw, I just remembered that I have to help my dad wash the car," Eric said, shifting his weight from one foot to another.

"You aren't leaving!" Mallory said and got into his friend's face. "Maybe, I should hang you up there, instead?"

"Cool out, man. I'm staying."

Caleb took advantage of the two arguing and managed to slip his head out of the noose, grab a low-hanging branch, and pull himself up. He started climbing as fast as he could.

"Dammit, he's getting away!" Mark said.

Eric looked up at the tree and shook his head. "No way. I don't like heights."

Mark raised his balled fist to Eric's face. "Get up there, or I'm gonna beat your scrawny ass worse than I'm gonna beat his. It was your fault he got away."

Eric sighed.

Caleb was already halfway up the forty-foot-tall oak tree when he looked down to find a nervous Eric not far below him. This made him start climbing faster.

"When you catch him, I want you to push him out of the tree!" Mallory yelled.

A wild breeze whipped through the tree, and Eric nearly lost his footing. He re-established his bearings, but the fear was in his eyes.

"Jesus, I hate heights," he mumbled to himself and was just about to resume his climb when something invisible moved a large branch a few feet from his outstretched right hand.

"What are you doing? You almost got him!" Mallory yelled, waving his arms.

"No way! I'm not climbing that high!" Eric said as he awkwardly turned to start the journey back down, still freaked out by the moving branch.

Caleb heard a flutter and caught the glimpse of a shadow hit Eric hard on his right shoulder. This caused the bully to fall a few branches; he managed to grab onto a smaller one to keep from tumbling all the way to the ground, but the slender limb bent badly from his weight. He knew it wouldn't hold him for much longer.

"Help me!" Frame called.

"What am I supposed to do down here?" Mark yelled back. "Just grab something, dumbass!"

Caleb saw the dread in Eric's eyes as his red fingers tried to remain clutched onto the thin branch. Slowly, an invisible force peeled each one of Eric's fingers from the branch until he had no grip left and tumbled down violently, landing with a hard thud in front of a wide-eyed Mark.

"Oh, shit … you okay?" Mark asked.

A bloodied Eric slowly got to his feet, holding his left arm. "I think I broke it. My parents are gonna kill me."

"He did this!" a red-faced Mallory said, pointing into the treetop.

"Let's just go," Frame pleaded.

Caleb still clung to the treetop, but he let go with one hand to raise a middle finger at Mark.

"You'll pay for this *Clay Boy*!" Mark said. "If you think this is over, you're fucking stupider than you look!"

Caleb waited until they were long gone before starting the descent, but he couldn't shake the feeling that someone was watching him from the trees.

"Hello? Is a-anybody there?"

Caleb thought he caught a glimpse of a shadow from the corner of his eye, but it quickly vanished among the dense branches. He bent over to wash the blood from his scraped legs and caught the reflection of a dark-haired boy in the bubbling stream. It looked just like how he imagined Gren in his mind. He was smiling.

22

From Paranormal vs. Science Magazine, 2015
"Invisible Friends Among Us" – by Doctor Barry Tenzin Dorjee, PhD

Vanderbilt University Department of Psychology and Child Development conducted a survey of a thousand children across the United States. While invisible friends are not a normal topic in a scientific study, this phenomenon is not uncommon. According to the survey, forty percent of children will have an imaginary friend by the time they're ten. The University of Oregon also found similar instances, discovering that thirty-eight percent of children will have an imaginary friend by age seven.

These invisible friends most commonly make their appearance between the ages of three and five. And while most are human in appearance—and interestingly, usually the same gender as the child who created them—over half the kids did not imagine just human invisible friends: some were cartoon characters and animals. Some of the children were recorded on video, and went into detail about their friends:

Heather, age 7: "She's a kitty cat. She likes to turn on the TV and push me around on my bicycle. My mom gets mad when the TV comes on in the middle of the night, but it's always my friend Kitty Cat."

Bethany Ann, age 12: "My friend is named Mopsey. He was my stuffed animal, but now he is alive, like me and you. He helps me to not be sad.

Interviewer: "Why are you sad?"

Bethany Ann: "A monster lives in my closet. He comes out at night. My stuffed Mopsey protects me. I talked to him all the time, and I imagined him talking back to me. Then, one day, he did talk back to me."

Bethany Ann was an earlier patient of my own, a girl about Caleb's age. She had created this imaginary friend to deal with abuse from her father. She was ultimately placed in a mental health center, a ward of the state, after her mother supposedly murdered her father in alleged defense of her daughter.

Bethany Ann's experiences were very different from the rest of the children's. Bethany was a lot older, and she spoke about Mopsey's point of view, and the way he experienced emotions. I had a strong hunch that what she was describing was not an imaginary friend, but a Tulpa. I believed then, as I believe now, that it was her Tulpa who killed her father by pushing him down the stairs. Over the course of our time together, I would learn that I was correct in my assumption and it would change the direction of my life and career.

I have documented several cases of people being possessed by their Tulpa. The possession can differ between switching in the short term, in which the host doesn't necessarily experience a time loss, and a type where the Tulpa takes control of a part or all of the host's body completely, leaving a gaping hole in the person's memory. I have not witnessed this firsthand, but Bethany was very upset when talking about this place she called Wonder Farm. Her time there was lasting longer and longer, and she was starting to have no sense of just how long she had been away.

23

Ole Bill Hall sat on his porch, glancing from his dusty field back to his coffee mug. The sky was a vibrant painting of reds and purples. He grunted a curse under his breath about the afternoon heat while maneuvering the cup in his good hand to get a better grip on its chipped handle. He took a sloppy gulp and looked out over his cemetery of rusty farm equipment. There were multiple combine harvesters, cotton pickers, discs, and even an old Coke delivery truck.

He and his wife had been married for thirty-one years when she vanished while hanging clothes on a line behind the house. One minute she was there, and the next, she was gone. People around town often speculated that she may have been a victim of the *Cove Strangler*, but she didn't fit the description of his other victims. Bill would often tell his neighbors that he thought she might of run off with an old boyfriend from college.

Bill's eyes narrowed as he spied Caleb crossing through his field: he didn't like it one damn bit. He had told the boy time and again that his collection of farm equipment was no jungle gym, but here he was jumping the fence and heading for the old combine. Bill couldn't believe his eyes, but deep down was kind of impressed that the boy was brave enough to be there, especially when Ole Gruff was around. He watched the boy stare at the ground, combing through the tall weeds, looking for something. He hated nosy people and trespassers. That's why he had trained the goat to be meaner than your average billy goat.

The farmer could see Caleb popping up every few seconds to make sure the goat wasn't around, making him smile. A little show was about to happen because he could see Ole Gruff was grazing not too far away. He stood, placed his fingers in his mouth, and let out a loud whistle.

"*Weeeeeh!* Dinner time, Gruff!"

The goat's head shot up, and he spotted Caleb.

Caleb heard the call and began searching more frantically. He finally spotted the red leather of his glove in the tall grass. It lay beside a rusted rotary combine harvester.

"You're right; it *was* here," Caleb said to his invisible friend.

The combine's once vibrant fire-engine-red paint was now the color of a ripe tomato, and for years birds had nested in its rusted-out guts. The front windshield had a jagged crack that road-mapped down into the paint-flaked valley of its warped metal hood.

The busted windows looked like the jagged teeth of a hungry monster. Caleb started climbing up fast because he knew the goat was coming. He pulled himself inside the cab and tried to pull the door closed, but it was broken and wouldn't budge. He placed his hands on the huge steering wheel. "I wish I had the k-keys," he said, craning his neck from one murky window to the next, trying to spot Ole Gruff. Billies can climb steep surfaces fairly easily, and Caleb knew this.

A meaty hand suddenly grabbed a surprised Caleb by the shoulder and jerked him down onto the side panel of the machine.

"What I tell you 'bout climbing on this stuff, boy?" Bill Hall shouted at the cowering Caleb. The man rarely bathed, and his body and breath reeked of alcohol and rotten food. The scent mixed with the heat of the day made the boy dizzy.

"I was l-looking for my g-glove."

"Well, looks like you found it, so get on before I feed you to Gruff!"

The terrified boy ran like he was on fire, and the fence was water.

"I best not catch you out here again!" Bill shouted after him.

Caleb cleared the fence and kept running. When he stopped to catch his breath, something caught his eye—a set of keys hanging from a low branch. Caleb slid the keys from the limb and saw a Kellogg's *Cereal Rooster* on the faded yellow rubber key chain.

24

The freshly mowed baseball diamond seemed to glow as several players lazily warmed up for afternoon practice. Caleb stood on the other side of the fence, proudly holding the glove Coach Darter had given him and that he had just won back from the clutches of a monster goat. He bent down, mimicked a snatch of a ground ball, and pretended to throw it to first base because none of the other kids would pair up with him. He looked stiff and uncoordinated, but his enthusiasm shone through.

Mark Mallory crashed shoulders with Caleb as he ran onto the field. "You lost, Clay Boy?" Mark asked, placing a baseball bat horizontally behind his head, rotating his body from side to side.

"C-Coach Darter told me to come."

"No way," Mark said to Eric Frame, who now wore a cast on his arm. "Claytards don't play baseball, right, Eric?"

Eric just nodded but didn't say anything. He couldn't really do much in his cast, but practice was mandatory. He looked scared, and Caleb noticed this shift in the bully/victim dynamic; he kind of liked it. It was the same shift that his uncle had gone through.

"Then don't be such a chicken-shit and warm up with us," Mallory said as he tossed the ball to his pal, Eric.

"Why are you so quiet?" Mark asked his friend, throwing the ball harder.

"I'm just focused on practice."

"You're scared of that wimp, aren't you?"

"What? Hell no!"

"You are. I can see it in your eyes when you look at him. What happened in that tree?"

Eric shook his head. "There's something not right about him."

"Watch this. Hey, one of your shoes is untied!"

Caleb looked down as the ball came hard from Mark, hitting the boy square in the chest. It punched the breath out of him and sent him to the ground like instant cement. He gasped for breath like a fish out of water.

The other boys stood in silence, waiting for Caleb's reaction.

"Oops! Sorry 'bout that, I thought you were paying attention," Mallory said and rolled his head as if to show concern. "You're not supposed to catch a ball with your body. Maybe, we should get some help for the little guy?"

Coach Darter stepped out of the dugout to see about the ruckus. "What's going on out here, Mallory? Frame?"

"Uh, I dunno. Caleb Jenkins missed a catch and got hurt," Mallory said in the most innocent voice he could muster.

"You okay, Caleb?" Coach Darter asked.

The hurt was subsiding enough for Caleb to try to stand.

"It was just an accident, right Jenkins?" Mallory said.

"Uh, y-yeah," a still out-of-breath Caleb said as the coach helped him up the rest of the way.

"It better have been an accident. And what happened to your arm, Frame?" Coach Darter asked.

Eric rolled his head and held up his broken arm. "I fell off my dirt bike."

"We're playing Decatur next week! How are we ever gonna win State with you all acting like this?" Sam took off his cap, tossed it on the ground, and gave it a good kick.

"Sorry, Coach," Eric said.

"It's not just you, Frame … it's all of you! I thought you might be tired of losing all the time, but maybe not."

"I wanna win State, coach!" Mark said.

"Well, then start acting like it. Start acting like a team. You sure you're okay, Caleb?"

Caleb nodded.

"Walk it off. Let's take batting practice. Mallory, you're pitching. Eric, you need to sit this one out, and Caleb—you're in the box."

"Me?"

"Yeah, show 'em you're here to play ball."

"Watch me strike this fool out," Mallory told Eric.

Mark took the mound, flipped off Caleb, and then mouthed the word *asshole*.

Coach Darter put his hand on Caleb's shoulder. "I want you to try and read the writing on that baseball as it comes toward you. Don't take your eyes off the ball, got it?"

The first pitch came close to Caleb's face and caused him to fall backward and into the dirt. Mark smiled his classic asshole smile. "Nobody crowds *my* plate."

"That's enough, Mallory," Coach said.

Caleb stood and dusted himself off. He tapped the bottom of his cleats with the tip of his bat and squared up.

The second pitch came right down the pipe.

Caleb swung his bat high and spun all the way around.

"Strike one!" the red-haired catcher yelled.

"Keep your eye on the ball. Your head was way over here," Coach said.

The third pitch was a change-up. Caleb managed to get a small piece of the ball, but it went foul, up and over the back wall.

"Strike two!" Eric shouted.

"Okay, Frame, we can do without the play-by-play!" Coach yelled. "Alright, Caleb, you got this!" he said, clapping.

"Better get used to riding the bench, Clay Boy," Frame said low in a low voice.

Mark came hard with a fastball right down the middle.

Caleb connected and sent a laser beam right back at Mark, hitting him in the nuts. Mallory went down like a sack of bricks.

"Oh, damn!" Coach Darter blurted out.

Caleb was frozen for a second before realizing he had made contact.

Coach and the others went to check on Mark, who moaned in pain.

"You need to take a trip to the school nurse, Mallory?"

"No, I'm alright."

"S-sorry," Caleb said.

"You're gonna be," Mark said as he limped off the field.

25

Lois Jenkins made her way down the wide aisles of the local Piggly Wiggly, buying food for her church's Sunday potluck. She hated the store for many reasons. For one, this was where Sheriff Darter had told her they found her sister's body back in 2009. Since then, the store's scent of stale milk and newspaper print hung over her head like a dark cloud. No matter what she did, she just couldn't wash it away from her mind.

She grabbed what she needed and hurried to the checkout line. She knew the longer she was here, the more likely she would have a run-in with a *caring* neighbor. It was just a way for them to obtain ammo for their gossip.

Lois had gathered a week's worth of groceries and was attempting to checkout when she glanced over at today's copy of the *Wheeler Gazette*. A high school photo of her sister was on the cover, with the headline: "*Has the Cove Strangler Returned to Wheeler's Cove?*"

Lois suddenly felt like she was under water, as she opened the paper to the article and started reading:

HAS THE COVE STRANGLER RETURNED?

Local Wheeler middle school teacher Mary Cardin's body was found in woods just West of Wheeler Middle School early Sunday morning, strangled. An officer responded around 7 a.m. after a local man, Bill Hall, called 911. Local sheriffs were called to the scene but were unable to determine who the attacker was. There are similarities to a rash of killings that took place here back in the two-thousands by a serial killer known as the Cove Strangler. The last of his victims was a local girl and former Wheeler Diamond Queen, Claire Conroy. This killer was never brought to justice. Police and the local Sheriff's Department ask anyone with information about this active criminal investigation to contact the department hotline.

All of the old fears and terror of losing her sister seemed to fall from the ceiling like deadweight. The checkout line started to blur, and people's faces became exaggerated.

"Are you okay, ma'am?" a concerned sack boy asked. His voice sounded like it was in slow motion.

Whispers filled her ears as the ground pulsed and rippled.

Lois placed a hand on the candy rack for balance but pulled it down instead. The giant glass jar of pickles that she held slipped out of her fingers and exploded in dozens of shards on the hard tile.

Every person in the store stopped and stared. She could hear them whispering like they had used to whisper when her sister was first murdered.

"Ma'am, are you alright?" a young checkout girl asked.

"Yes, I mean, no," Lois said as she bent over to pick up a large piece of glass. She held it between her fingers, staring.

"Just leave it, hon. I'll get one of the boys to sweep that up."

"I-I didn't mean to," she said, placing the shard of glass in her purse and walking out.

The checkout girl picked up the store intercom. "Clean-up at station three," she said and shook her head.

Once Lois was in her car, she pulled the shard of glass from her purse and held it up to the light. Huge tears welled up in her red eyes, and she screamed, punching the steering wheel over and over.

An overweight woman appeared at her window. "You alright, darling?"

Lois angrily rolled down her window. "Mind your own damn business!"

"Pardon me? I was just trying to help."

The actual concern in the woman's eyes calmed Lois. She recognized the woman's face from her most recent vision. She was lying dead, surrounded by dozens of townspeople. The middle school was burning in the background. "I'm sorry. I'm sorry." Lois threw the shard of glass to the floorboard, started up her car, and peeled out of the parking lot.

It wasn't only the return of her sister's suspected killer that had her upset, but also the dream that she had of the tornado that was going to hit Wheeler's Cove in a few days. Her husband had not told his congregation the entire story because he didn't know it. Nestor wouldn't be this renowned prophet without her special ability. She had torn out a second page from her sketch pad. The missing page showed an image of a monster, and that monster resembled Caleb, but it's face was scarred and distorted.

26

From *Ancient Voices Within Us All: A Study of Tulpamancery* by Doctor Barry Tenzin Dorjee, PhD, page 51:

Science has proven that our thoughts and decisions come down to different molecules (a slight electric current with a varying charge gradient.). I have administered a ball-drop PK test to many patients who claim to have created a Tulpa. This test rates levels of influence on an object or a physical process using the power of the mind.

In the test, I drop a ball, and it is deflected to the left or right by a series of pins as it falls. The subject attempts to use their psychokinetic ability (thoughts) to move the ball one way or another. My recent patient, Caleb Jenkins, managed to move the ball to the right sixty percent more than to the left, which eliminates the 'random' movements of the ball and indicates to me the presence of strong psychokinetic ability. The results prove that subjects who have created powerful Tulpas in mere weeks (a feat that takes decades for advanced Vajrayana Buddhists and mystics) are, in fact, omnikinetic Tulpamancers.

27

Clouds of tiny gnats gathered under the stadium lights as they shone over the well-groomed Wheeler Middle School ball field. Small groups of locals headed to their seats in the aluminum bleachers. If the Wheeler Wildcats won tonight, they would face the Champion Decatur Crimson Bulls for their Homecoming next Friday. This community loved their baseball, but the stands were emptier than usual, except for the hardcore few.

The news of the Cove Strangler's new victim had hit the local papers and evening news. It had everyone spooked. The boogeyman of Wheeler had returned to this God-fearing community, and too many remembered the fear that gripped them years ago. It was a story that made national headlines and affected every member of the community in its own unique way.

Coach Darter was in the dugout looking over the team roster and obsessively chomping on a piece of gum. The smell of the baseball field was like a time machine. He thought back to his first season as a Los Angeles Dodger. It was bittersweet to see his dream finally come true, only to have it crushed by an injury in the first season of what looked like a promising career. The team would go on to defeat the Colorado Rockies in the National League West tie-breaker game to claim their sixth straight NLW Championship, but ultimately lose the World Series to Boston Red Sox.

"Keep your eye on the ball," he said and clapped.

Sam was brought in to close a mid-season game against the Oakland Athletics. They were down by three in the eighth. This was only Sam's third trip to the mound. He still wasn't used to the roar of the crowd.

His first pitch was high and to the left.

"Ball!" the ref yelled, as the thunderbolt of a pitch slapped the glove.

A steely eyed Sam took in the next sign from the catcher. He calmed his mind, but for some reason his father's voice was loud in his head. He was suddenly a little boy again. A little boy that could do nothing right. A little boy who would never escape the Corny Cove.

He reared back and threw another bolt.

"*Strike!*" the ump shouted. The ball slapped the glove.

Sam flinched. The sound brought back memories of his father and mother fighting. The terrible anger that his father had. The sound of slapping he would hear while lying in bed at night. He would pull the sheets up over his head, but he could still hear the slaps.

"*Strike!*" The ump yelled.

Sam removed his hat and wiped the sweat from his brow. His pitching arm felt like a limp noodle. He knew that he shouldn't throw another pitch, but he had to show everyone what he was made of. He had to show the little town of Wheelers Cove that he wasn't a scared little kid. He had to show his father that he was a winner.

The sign came.

Sam wound up for the pitch.

He released it like a bullet from a gun, but as he did, he heard his shoulder pop.

"*Strike Three!*"

The batter was out, and so was Sam.

"Coach," a player said, breaking Sam out of his memory.

"Uh?"

"Your cell phone is ringing."

"Oh, thanks," he said, and answered it. "Hello, Darter here."

"Dad? You still need me to keep the books at the game?"

"Hey, baby, I do kinda need your help over here, if you don't mind. Did you have other plans?"

"I was going to hang out at the local video store with a new friend, but I can go after the game."

Sam let out a long sigh. "Are you asking my permission or telling me?"

"Uh, asking. Please?" Helen said. He could almost see her wrinkling her nose.

"Who is this new friend?"

"A guy who works at the local video store. He's just a friend."

"How old is this guy?" he asked.

"Sixteen."

"That's two years older than you, and it's not safe to be out after dark for a while."

"It hasn't been safe for a while. I'm a big girl, dad."

"I'll explain to you later, but I need you here."

"I'm on my way," she said. "What's wrong with you?"

"I ran into my dad today."

"Oh, shit. How did that go?"

"Watch the language!" Sam said and took off his ball cap to run his fingers through his hair. "Awkward. I told him I didn't want him to get to know you, but now that I think about it, I guess that should be up to you."

"I don't want to if you don't want me to."

"Let's talk in person about this, but please hurry up and get over here."

"On my way. Love you, Dad!"

"Love you too," he said and hung up the phone. He let out a long sigh and wondered if coming back here was a bad mistake. He was usually good at just 'rolling with the flow,' but seeing his father really messed with his head and emotions. He felt like that helpless kid, again, and never wanted to put his daughter through that. He looked out over the bright green and smiled. This game had gotten him through some hard times.

28

Caleb sat in his uncle's car with his glove in his lap and a ball of clay in his hands. He was filled to the brim with uncertainty and shaping the clay always helped. "Why d-did you change your mind about letting me p-play?"

"Your aunt wanted you to have the opportunity. She thought it would be a good way to make friends, so I changed my mind." Nestor looked nervous, and he was careful with his words.

"O-okay," Caleb said and got out of the car, slamming the door behind him.

Caleb's uncle rolled down his window. "Uh, wait!" he said awkwardly. "I'll come back in a few hours to pick you up, if you want me to?"

"I'd rather w-walk home," Caleb said as his shoulders sunk. He looked out onto the field filled with other ball players. He gripped the clay mass in his hand and stuck it into his pocket.

"I guess that's alright," his uncle said. "Hey, since you got a glove already, I got something else for you," he said, reaching into the backseat.

He leaned out the window and handed Caleb a wooden baseball bat.

"It's w-wooden?"

"Yeah, just like the pros use. I'm proud of you, Caleb. God is proud of you."

"They use a-aluminum bats in middle school."

"I found it at a yard sale. Thought you'd like it, but if you don't …"

"Th-thanks," Caleb said and started walking toward the gate that led to the dugout.

"Hey, wait."

Caleb stopped and turned.

"Maybe, I've treated you too harshly over the years."

"G-Gren says you don't mean that," Caleb said, walking back to the window, while tightly gripping the handle of the bat.

"H-hey, t-take it easy."

Caleb leaned in close to his uncle. "Look who's stuttering, now."

Nestor frantically started the car and drove off in a cloud of gravel smoke.

A hand snatched Caleb's wooden bat away. "Nice bat. Looks like you can barely lift it?" Mallory scoffed. "And don't think I forgot that I owe you an ass-kicking."

"G-give it back," Caleb said, trying to grab his bat.

"Make me, you little pussy," Mark taunted to the laughs of the other boys, as well as that of Mark's cheerleader girlfriend, Lexi.

She took off Caleb's hat and tossed it over to Eric. "Fly, little birdie!"

"Throw it here!" Mark yelled at Eric, standing off to the side.

Eric tossed the hat back to Caleb with his good hand.

"What's your deal?" Mark asked.

"I … I don't think we should mess with him anymore," Eric said, avoiding eye contact with Mark.

"You're starting to stutter like that retard. I want you to take this bat and hit him with it!" Mark held out the bat.

"No, no way," Eric said.

Caleb closed his eyes and cringed in anticipation of the blow, but it never came, and as he slowly opened them, he saw Bill Hall holding the bat. The Frankenstein's Monster of a man wore his standard costume: overalls and a wide-brimmed Madewell with frayed edges. "You boys up to no good, ain't ya?"

The bullies stood frozen under the shadow of the giant farmer.

"Everything okay over here?" asked Mark's father, Jack Mallory, as he walked up with a bag of equipment.

Mark smiled, knowing his father would take his side. "Old Man Hall pushed me down because my ball accidentally hit this kid. Eric and me were just warming up with a game of pepper."

"That true, Bill? You put your hands on my kid?" Jack said, dropping his bag of gear and preparing to fight, which showed just how stupid the Mallory family was. "You know that I was the one who asked the school board to let you raise the flag before games; everyone else didn't want you here."

"Your boy, and his friends, were picking on this one," Bill said.

"Sometimes balls hit people," Jack Mallory said. "Don't you ever lay hands on my kid again, or I will get you banned from this ball field. Do you understand me?" The angry father tapped the giant's chest with his middle finger to make his point.

"I don't like it when people point their fingers at me," Bill growled softly as he loomed over the much smaller Jack Mallory.

"Tough shit," Jack squealed, suddenly conscious of what he might have done, picking on the huge farmer.

"He's an old asshole," Mark lipped while picking up a handful of gravel to throw at Bill Hall.

"Shut your mouth, Mark. Let's go!" Shaking, Jack walked away, dragging his son along with him.

"You okay, boy?" Bill asked Caleb as he extended a hand.

"Yeah."

Caleb squirmed under Bill Hall's hard gaze.

"Th-thank you," Caleb said.

Bill's face softened. "You're welcome. I'm your friend."

A jealous Gren stirred within Caleb. "*You're not my friend. I know what happened to your wife*," Caleb said without stuttering, and in a deeper voice.

"What did you just say, boy?"

"I d-didn't say it."

"You messing with me, you weird little shit?" Bill fidgeted.

"My f-friend knows things."

"So, where's this friend, now?

"He does not like t-talking to p-people."

"Is he on the ball team with you?" Bill asked, looking around at the other boys warming up on the field.

"No, he lives in the woods."

"You better stop playing games and tell me where this friend is. There ain't no boy who lives in the woods."

"N-no, I am t-telling the truth."

"You might want to tell that friend of yours to mind his own goddamn business, or something bad is gonna happen to him and you," Bill said, pinching Caleb's shoulder hard.

"Ouch, you are h-hurting me." Caleb squirmed under the pain.

"Pain helps ya remember things," Bill said, glaring down at him. "And you best remember what I told ya."

"My friend does not like it when p-people hurt me."

"Oh, is that so? You can tell your little fr—"

Bill let Caleb go as a parent walked by and smiled. The old farmer took off his hat and nodded like a perfect gentleman. "How ya doing, ma'am. Good night for a ball game, ain't it?"

Bill Hall put his hat back on and leaned back into Caleb. "Your little fucking friend and me are gonna have a talk real soon. Count on it!"

Caleb glared at the farmer, then smiled. "He kn-knows."

Two: Destruction

29

Both teams were standing midfield, with their hats off, as the National Anthem finished. A scowling Eric Frame sat on the bench with a cast on his arm.

Mark had convinced him they would look pretty bad in front of the others if they told anyone that Caleb the Clay Boy had gotten the better of him.

Coach Darter had put Caleb on third base.

Caleb punched the inside of his glove a few times. Mark Mallory was pitching for the Wildcats.

"Let's go, Cats!" Eric yelled.

Caleb was nervous because he only got a chance to warm up and hadn't even been to a practice yet. The batter that was up was a giant kid and was known for hitting rifled line drives down the third base line.

"Caleb, look sharp!" Coach Darter yelled.

"Batter! Batter! Swing!" the infield chanted over and over as Ky Buck stepped to the plate, tapping his cleats with his bat.

The first pitch was a hard knock-foul ball down the third baseline. The stocky batter smirked at the pale-looking Caleb, who was still amazed at how fast the ball had zoomed past.

"It's coming at you!" the batter announced and nodded at Caleb.

Caleb punched his fist into his mitt and dug his feet in, awaiting the next pitch.

The batter connected and sent a laser of a line drive toward Caleb, who opened his glove wide at just the right time to catch the ball.

Coach Darter went wild with excitement. "Holy cow! Did you see that?" He threw his hat into the air and jumped up and down.

Caleb opened his eyes and held up the glove with the ball sitting inside.

"I did it," Caleb said to himself. "I c-caught it."

"Lucky catch," Mark scoffed and kicked the dirt.

"Way to go, Caleb!" a female voice came from the outfield.

Caleb looked over at the dugout to see Helen waving her arms.

"You rock, Caleb Jenkins! Woo-hoo!" she yelled and did a little dance to the stares of locals and the outfield players.

Helen spotted her grandfather out in the lot behind center field. He was leaning on the front of the police cruiser, wearing a pair of mirrored sunglasses. He raised his hand and gave the thumbs up.

"Granddad?" Helen asked.

"Yeah, your mom suggested you get to know him, but I'll leave that up to you."

Helen shrugged. "I know you don't like him, and you've never told me why, not exactly."

"I don't want to get into that here, but he wasn't a good man."

"Maybe he's changed."

"Doubtful," Sam said and spat his gum into the trash.

"Thanks, Dad."

"For what?"

"Talking to me like an adult. I'm going to go introduce myself."

"Jenkins!" Coach yelled.

"Y-Yes, sir."

"Walk with my daughter."

"Okay," Caleb said and smiled.

Helen and Caleb made their way out to where her granddad was.

"You played a great game. You going for pizza after?"

Caleb suddenly got nervous. "I-I don't think so."

"Yes, you are," Helen said, putting her arm around him. Caleb blushed.

"O-okay."

"So, that's settled."

"I heard that Sh-sheriff is Coach's dad?"

"Yeah, and my grandfather. I've never met him. That's weird, right?"

"Why is that w-weird? I live with my s-super religious aunt and uncle b-because my mother was killed by a psycho."

Sheriff Darter removed his sunglasses and smiled when he saw Helen.

"Wait here. I'll be right back," she told Caleb.

Caleb nodded his head and let her walk over by herself.

"Oh, my sweet Lord. I think I see an angel. I know you gotta be Helen. You look like a Darter," he said, opening his arms wide to hug her.

"Hi," she said sheepishly and hugged him back.

"You are beautiful, just beautiful!" He ran his hand through her hair. "I guess your dad's not coming to say hello?"

She shook her head.

"Well, our problems are not your problems. So, tell me what you think of our little town?"

"Well, it is little. I like the video store."

"You doing okay in school?"

"So far, so good."

"You got a boyfriend yet?"

She shook her head, embarrassed. "Maybe?"

"Well, it's better not to rush into things. I know your little escort, here. Good to see you, Mr. Jenkins. How are your aunt and uncle?"

"F-fine," he said.

"Your mother being murdered was a horrible tragedy for this town."

"Wait, you told me your mother was killed, she was murdered?"

"I thought your dad would have told you. She was murdered by a serial killer—the Cove Strangler."

Helen's face dropped as she turned to see if Caleb had heard what her grandfather had said.

Huge tears were pouring down the boy's cheeks.

Chatter from his police radio: *"Sheriff, you there?"*

"You shouldn't have said that in front of him."

"Hold on a sec, Helen," he said and reached through his open window to grab his walkie. "Marcus here. What's up?"

"We have a problem that needs your attention over at the Hall Farm."

"Uh, be right there," he said and turned to Helen. "I gotta go. Duty calls."

"People are saying they found another dead girl? Is that true?"

"I can't really talk about that, but let's keep this going. Stop by the station, and we can go for ice cream. I'll even take you for a ride in my cruiser."

"I'm fourteen, now."

"We can do whatever you want."

Helen had already walked away.

"Talk to you soon, angel!" he said and left.

Helen turned to Caleb.

"Are you okay?"

Caleb was shaking. He nodded. "Th-that's what my d-dreams are about."

She hugged him.

30

Sam pulled his Jeep Cherokee into the circular driveway of his two-story brick home in the fancy gated community of Falcon's Ridge. It was on the more affluent side of town and a stone's throw from a premier golf course. It had a large dock with a boat slip just down the hill from the bright-green backyard. Sam's brand-new pontoon bobbed up and down on the waters of Lake Chasten. The sinking sun was just over the treetops on the other side of the water, making the scenery look like a postcard that you find on vacation that says: *Wish You Were Here*. He'd spent many summers on that lake, boating and fishing, and had always wanted a house there. He and Marie looked at many properties in town, but they instantly fell in love with this one.

He got out of his car and sighed. He'd been so busy with his team and school that he hadn't let it all soak in. "Welcome home, Sam," he said to himself and smiled.

Inside, Marie was fixing the table, but she didn't look happy. Two tall candles flickered beside plates and wine glasses.

"You're early. Did we win?" she said with a sharp tone. She fastened a gold hoop earring.

Sam sighed. "Okay, what did I do now? I know our anniversary isn't until next month, so what is it?"

"I thought we could use a romantic meal," she said, cocking her head, nearly in tears. "I was having a hard time remembering the last time we had one, but then I found this," she said, pulling a cell phone from her apron. "When did you get a secret cell phone?"

"That's a student's phone. I meant to leave it at school."

"What?"

"I confiscated it from a student named Eric Frame. He and some friends were bullying the Jenkins boy. I just forgot to give it back."

Her face dropped. "Oh, I guess I'm acting cra cra!"

"No, you are not crazy," he took the phone gently, sat it on the table, and kissed her.

Her eyes were still filled with tears of embarrassment and expelled anger. "I just feel like we are ships passing in the night. I wanted tonight to be special."

"Sorry about that." He dropped his head a bit. It just dawned on him that he had been obsessed with building a winning team just as his old man was obsessed with finding a killer. Obsessive behavior ran in the family. Sam took the wine bottle from Marie's hand and sat it on the table. He then took her into his arms. "Damn, you smell good."

"I'm probably overly emotional because of my condition."

"What's your condition?"

"One that makes you go to the market in the middle of the night for pistachio ice cream."

Sam's face dropped. "Are you . . .?"

Happy tears flowed. "Yes."

He wiped her cheek and started kissing her.

"Tell me you're happy."

Sam pulled his head back and looked at her square in the face. "I'm the happiest man on the planet," he said and started taking her clothes off.

"What are you doing? Don't you wanna eat first? What if Helen walks in?"

"She's not gonna be home anytime soon. She's at a pizza place with a boy."

Marie turned to face him. They were close, their lips nearly touching. She frowned. "Wait, a boy? She didn't tell me anything about a boy."

"He's harmless. The Jenkins boy I was telling you about. She feels sorry for him. I don't think he has many friends."

"That's nice of her."

"You run into your father yet?"

Sam pulled back. "In town and at the ball field."

"And?" she asked with a cocked eyebrow.

"Same ole bullshit. He wants to see Helen, and I don't want him to," he said, grabbing the bottle and pouring a glass of wine.

"Okay, I guess we won't talk about it," she said and went back to setting the table. "But he is gonna be around. This town only has two grocery stores."

He grabbed her again and brought her to his chest. "He hurt me and my mother, real bad. I can see myself in him, and it messes me up thinking about it. I don't want to be anything like that man, and I don't want his poison infecting this family."

She caressed his cheek. "Baby, you're a good husband and father. You're nothing like him."

"I love you," he said and kissed her neck delicately.

"Well, I guess we are gonna have dessert before dinner?"

"Guess so," he said, and they both laughed.

The smoke alarm suddenly went off.

"Oh, damn. I had the rolls warming; it must be a little too warm. Hold that thought. I'll be right back."

He laughed, picked up the confiscated cell phone and accidentally opened it to a video of when the clay bird hit the substitute teacher in the face. He could see Caleb sitting at his desk and being pestered by Mark Mallory.

Caleb's eyes rolled back into his head as he held up the clay sculpture. The bird appeared to fly from his hand and hit the teacher in the face.

"What the hell?" He paused it for a moment and then rewatched the video again.

His wife walked back into the room. "Well, I guess we could order a pizza."

Sam was silent. In shock.

"What are you watching?"

"I'm not really sure."

31

Most of the kids from the ball field met at the Wagon Wheel after games. It was the home of the *Giant Pepperoni Wheel,* as the sign said. Caleb was pretty surprised that Helen asked him to go. No one had ever asked him to go anywhere.

Caleb and Helen were standing in the alleyway beside the pizza place.

Helen lit up a cigarette and was eyeing a nervous Caleb. "You're worried that Mark Mallory and his asshole friends are going to be in there, aren't you?"

"Y-yeah."

"You can't let those guys run your life. The more you show that you are scared, the more they will mess with you. Believe me, I've had to deal with my share of bullies."

"You smoke?"

"Yeah, I'm old school. Vaping is so lame. You know who puts out all of those anti-tobacco ads?"

"No."

"The same companies that make the vapes and the stop-smoking patch. It's all a scam to get more people to start vaping. True story. I started back in Los Angeles to calm my nerves. I used to go to this stuck-up private school where people were not too nice to me. You want to talk about bullies? Girls are much meaner than guys. I should have gone to therapy, but smoking helps. Oh, and do *not* tell my dad," She puffed and ducked behind a telephone pole, waving away smoke in a vain hope it would dissipate so as not to draw attention to her.

"My aunt takes me to d-doctors, but they c-can never decide what is wrong with me. This new one I'm going to seems pretty cool. I guess I'm just messed up from my m-mother being killed."

"Everyone is a little messed up, so I wouldn't worry too much about it."

"I'm a lot messed up," he said, reaching into his pocket to feel the hunk of clay he always carried with him. His anxiety lowered whenever he manipulated it.

"It's so funny that doctors and parents will put a kid on every anti-psychotic, brain-frying pharmaceutical known to man but then tell you that smoking tobacco is bad," she said as she flicked her butt into the parking lot and sighed. "Let's go get us a wheel of pizza!"

"If I tell you a s-secret, you promise to not think I am c-crazy?"

"Of course."

"I have an imaginary f-friend."

"Aren't you a little old to have one of those?"

"He started out imaginary, but n-now he's not"

Helen laughed a little, not thinking he was serious, but he wasn't smiling. "You're just trying to scare me, right? You know I like scary movies, and you are trying to mess with my head. I'm impressed; I didn't know you had it in you."

"I'm not p-playing. My friend pushed Eric F-Frame out of a tree. That's why his arm is in a c-cast."

"I like this friend already. What do you mean *he* pushed? Is this like you summoned a ghost or a demon?"

"No, a T-Tulpa."

"What's an *Olpa*?"

"No, a *Tul-pa!* It is a p-person you create in your m-mind that becomes real the more you think about them. He has his own p-personality."

"Okay, color me intrigued. Prove it! Is he around us right now?"

"He does not like s-strangers."

"Then how can I be sure you're not bullshitting me?"

"He stays in the w-woods where it's quiet."

"Okay, why can't you take me there?"

Caleb thought about this for a minute.

"He says you can meet him if you go to the Diamond Dance with me after the Homecoming game," Caleb said, with a voice that sounded deeper and more confident.

"You didn't stutter."

"W-what?"

"You didn't stutter. And you can communicate with him?"

Caleb nodded his head. "We c-can hear each other's thoughts."

"Either you have the best imagination, or you're telling the truth. Ok, I'll go with you to the stupid Diamond Dance, even if you don't show me the crazy thing in the woods, but I'd also like to see the crazy thing in the woods."

"R-really?" Caleb asked with a huge smile on his face.

"You sure this is not a boy trick to get me into the woods?"

"Boy trick?" he said, looking confused.

"Never mind, what's your friend's name?"

"His name is Gren."

"That's creepy."

"He's named after G-Grendel, like from the story *Beowulf*."

"Okay. You named him?"

"No, he named himself."

"Wait, did a guy named Scares put you up to this?"

"Who is th-that?"

"He's this guy who works at the video store. He's into horror and makes movies. I'll introduce you. I just wanted to make sure."

32

The bell above the front door of the Giant Pepperoni rang like a loud gong. Everyone in the place turned to stare at Caleb and Helen, like in an old western movie when the gunslinger walks into the local saloon.

The place hadn't changed since the seventies. It had a certain charm to it and had been the hang-out for the young people of Wheeler's Cove since it first opened its doors. There was one of those stained-glass low-hanging lamps over a pool table, and a coin-operated machine dispensed the plastic balls with fake rings and stickers inside. The two-person Pac-Man cocktail table sat near the salad bar but hadn't worked since the late '80s.

"Wow, they let anyone in here!" Mark Mallory said, just loud enough for everyone to hear.

Helen walked by and flipped them the bird. "Just in case you forgot what your I.Q. was."

"Whoa, the new girl is raw," Lexi said.

Caleb was looking down, as usual.

"Ignore the lame, and let's get a slice. I still can't believe you made that badass catch," Helen said.

Scares was at the counter, already ordering.

"Hey, if it isn't the VHS Horror Meister himself! I thought I might see you at the ball game?" Helen said.

"Oh, I got caught up in discussion with a fellow horror aficionado about who is better: Jason or Michael?" he said as he took his greasy pizza slice and folded it up.

"What was the verdict?"

"Voorhees is indeed stronger, but let's not forget that *Friday the 13th* was inspired by *Halloween.* John Carpenter was ahead of his time. My vote was for Myers, a force of pure evil that kills everyone in his path just for the sake of killing. It's got that elemental thing to it."

"Yeah, but Jason was just a 'normal' kid who was left to die by camp counselors. He was a mama's boy. Jason is a more sympathetic character, and for that reason, more intriguing."

"Touché. Hey, I'm Scares," he said, holding out his fist to Caleb.

Caleb didn't get the social cue but nodded his head. "Hi, my name is C-Caleb."

Scares slowly reeled in his fist. "Okay, no worries. I gotta switch up my fist bump game."

Helen turned to Caleb. "Normally, on a date, the guy orders the food, but since I don't do normal, I'm ordering. You like extra pepperoni?"

"Did you say a d-date?" Caleb asked.

"Two giant slices with extra spicy pepperoni and two Cokes," Helen told the girl behind the register.

"My aunt and uncle don't like me drinking soda."

"Do you have to do everything your aunt and uncle want you to do?"

"N-no."

The girl ignored Helen, so she pulled herself up with her palms flat on the counter and yelled, "Two giant slices with extra pepperoni, *please*, and two large Cokes!"

The girl behind the counter heard but chose to ignore her. Instead, she grabbed two slices and walked them over to Mark Mallory's table. She bent over and hugged Mark's girlfriend, Lexi, and they both glanced up to see what kind of reaction they were getting out of Helen.

"Two monster slices coming up!" Scares said and jumped over the counter. He grabbed two slices from the hot case and threw them on plates. "I used to work here. The boss loved me, so these idiots won't say shit."

"My hero," Helen said.

Caleb could see that they had a connection, and the heat started to build inside of him.

They all sat in the corner of the pizza joint as Scares gave his take on everyone in the place. He was a walking gossip column of the town since everyone came into his store to rent movies.

"Okay, see the red-headed, rocker-wannabe bimbo sitting with Mark and Eric? Her name is Lexi Downy. She is the lead cheerleader in the pack that comes into the store every Friday night with the Hyenas. Rumor has it that she's already had plastic surgery. She's also a TikTok influencer."

"The Hyenas?" Helen asked.

"That's what everyone calls Mark Mallory and his group of assholes. They also have the worst taste in movies. The worst!" Scares said as he crammed another slice into his mouth. "They rent shit like *Fast & Furious 10*, whatever is popular and lame."

"You sure know a lot about students in a school you don't attend anymore," Helen said, sticking her tongue out at a leering Eric.

"I hate those troglodytes. I wanted to start a service for younger kids that is like bodyguards against assholes like them."

Mark got up and walked up to the counter. "Hey Helen, you want to hang out with someone besides these basics?"

"Do I hear something?" Helen said and acted like she was swatting a fly. "Kinda sounds like a fly buzzing around my head," she said, without looking at him. "They really should do something about the insect problem around here."

"You know you're hanging out with a straight-up perv, right? This guy was caught spying on the cheerleaders in their dressing room. There's a reason he's called Scares."

"That's not true, asshole," Scares said.

"He was hiding in one of the lockers," Mark said, bumping Scares to the side.

Helen looked at Scares. "I don't believe you," Helen said.

"I mean, if you're into freaks, we can definitely get freaky," Mark said, pinning Helen close to the counter.

Scares picked up a fork and, in one quick movement, held it to Mallory's eye. "Humans like you don't deserve to keep breathing."

Mark tensed up and raised a hand for protection. "Hey, don't go full psycho on me."

"I'll remove that eyeball and shove it up your ass!" Scares said.

"Scares, it's not worth it," Helen said.

The ceiling lights flickered.

Mark snatched the fork away from Scares and held it up to his throat. "You aren't talking tough, now?"

The lights flickered again. Caleb started to shake, as his eyes rolled in the back of his head.

"Caleb, are you okay?" Helen said when she noticed that he was rocking back in forth, with a zoned-out look on his face, as if he was in a trance.

One of the chairs near Caleb launched forward and hit Mark in the leg, which caused him to lose his balance and fall back. He clumsily tried grabbing the counter but instead snatched the edge of a plate with a slice of pizza, launching it into the air. It landed sauce-side up on Lexi's chest.

"Ugggh! My cheer uniform is ruined!" Lexi screamed as she stood and stormed out.

"Lexi, wait!" Mark yelled. "Dammit!" he roared and then turned back to Scares and Helen. "I'm gonna kill you, lames," he taunted and walked out after his girl.

"That's right! Keep walking!" Scares chimed in.

Scares grabbed Caleb's arm. "Hey, little guy—what's going on with him?"

"I don't know?"

Caleb's eyes fluttered open. "W-why is everyone staring at m-me?"

"Mark had a fork to Scare's throat, and you hit him with a chair." Helen said.

"I d-did?"

"Thank you, Sir Jenkins. You saved the damsel in distress; I'm talking about Scares," she said and lovingly punched Scares in the shoulder.

"Wait, I'm the damsel?"

Knowing Gren had tripped Mark somehow gave Caleb a boost of confidence. He felt like a normal kid eating pizza with friends.

"The whole Mallory crew should be put down for good. Too bad this isn't a horror movie. A monster would definitely jump out of the sewer system or the woods and rip them into little pieces," Scares said as he tore off a large chunk of pepperoni and devoured it.

A loud crack of thunder shook the windows of the pizza place. Caleb could see huge droplets of rain falling on the parked cars.

Scares, Helen, and Caleb stepped out the front door onto the sidewalk.

"This is going to be a fun walk to the woods," Helen sighed.

"You all still w-want to g-go?"

"Absolutely, Caleb!" Scares said.

"Th-Thanks."

"You don't need to thank us, we're your friends," Helen said.

"Not f-for that."

"What then?"

"For not c-calling me Clay B-boy."

Helen smiled.

Scares ran over to his van and slid open the side door. "Take a ride in the Scares express?"

"Caleb is taking me to see something amazing in the woods."

"Sure, okay? Well, I can give you a ride," Scares said, with his head cocked.

"N-no. We should walk," Caleb said.

"Does Gren care if Scares goes with us?"

"I d-don't know. He's not t-talking to me."

"Who minds?" Scares asked.

Helen's eyes got wide. She looked at Caleb. "Can I tell him?"

Caleb stared at Scares.

"Come on, I just held a fork up to Mark Mallory's eyeball for you. I wanna know why we are going to the woods in the rain."

"O-okay, you can come to meet Gren."

"Gren? Okay, I'm totally confused and totally curious," Scares said.

"Caleb said he made a Tulpa," Helen said.

"A what?"

"It's an entity generated by the mind."

Scares stopped walking. "You two are messing with me, right? What, like a spirit or something."

Caleb shook his head. "K-kinda"

Scares looked at Helen, who shrugged.

"I need to grab something out of my van."

33

From *Ancient Voices Within Us All: A Study of Tulpamancery* by Doctor Barry Tenzin Dorjee, PhD, Pg. 59:

There are many questions raised about Tulpas' power and ultimate potential. One question that I have encountered the most and even pondered at length is: are Tulpas the gods, angels, and demons that appear in our spiritual lexicon? Do humans create a sentient, supernatural world with our imaginations?

There is an occult concept of creating a distinct non-physical entity born from a collective group of people. This idea is called egregore but resembles what the Tulpamancers do when manifesting a Tulpa, except that this psychic thought-forming is done with a group of people. Does this not only explain deities but also faith healing, demonic possession, and stigmata?

The symbiotic event that happens between the group of worshipers and the egregore has been compared to the formation of a modern corporation (being recognized as a legal entity). These things are now created beings with rights like a real human, which is a pretty crazy thing to think about. Are they alive, in some sense?

The Tulpa is known to attach itself to a single person, but in some ultimate circumstances, they can become almost demonic, in the Christian sense of the word. They are capable of great evil, including jealousy, hate, and even murder. One of the most famous cases is The Slender Man, where two young girls imagined that an internet boogeyman was speaking to them, and, I think, believed in it so much that they created a Tulpa.

I'm not saying The Slender Man is real, I'm saying those little girls' Slender Man was real, and it instructed them to kill a neighbor girl by stabbing her over a dozen times and dumping her body in the woods. How real is Santa Claus, Easter Bunny, Old Man Winter, or the Bogeyman? Can we go even further and say the Greek Gods, Norse Gods, and possibly even present-day Gods are mental constructs? A product of millions and millions of focused imaginations?

Another famous case of a killer imaginary friend was the case of Mopsey and Bethany Ann. I testified as an expert witness for the defense in the case of a thirteen-year-old female patient of mine named Bethany Ann Laemmle. She was troubled due to horrific abuse perpetrated by her father. She created a Tulpa to cope with the trauma. Her creation was based on her favorite cartoon character—Mopsey the Pig. Her father was thrown off a flight of stairs and killed, and Bethany Ann's mother was convicted of his murder. I had been Bethany's therapist, and I was, and am, convinced it was Mopsey that killed her father. My biggest career regret at the time was I couldn't convince a jury of that.

34

The rain had started to come down hard as the three teens entered the edge of the woods. The drops thumped on the soft foliage and reverberated like hundreds of tiny drums.

"How far do we have to walk?" Helen said.

"I'm seeing some rad locations for my horror movie."

"J-just a little further. It's near the s-stream."

"Hiking in the rain is not what I thought I would be doing today," Scares said, raising his collar. "Should I be high for this? 'Cause, I'm thinking I need to be high for this. I thought you said you we were going to be talking to a ghost, so I brought my Ouija board from the van."

"You carry a Ouija board around with you?"

"Yeah, doesn't everybody?"

Caleb stopped at the edge of the tiny stream and looked up into the trees.

"Is he up in the trees?" Helen asked.

"Shush. We d-don't want to s-scare him off."

"This is crazy, right?" Helen said.

"I'm into it," Scares said.

"G-Gren?" Caleb called out.

"Does he smile a lot? Where did you come up with that?"

"G-R-E-N. He n-never smiles, except when we are alone in the woods."

"Gren!" Helen and Scares yelled, along with Caleb.

"Is he talking to you now?" Helen asked.

"What, he mentally communicates with you?"

"Yeah, I h-hear his voice in my h-head, sometimes. He's not t-talking to me now. I think he's mad because I b-brought you here."

"Well, let's try this," Scares said and pulled out the Ouija board from his satchel, which was covered in classic collectible monster, and punk band patches. "You said he's like a disembodied spirit with his own mind and personality, right? This is how we find out if you're just messing with us. If he communicates with you through telepathy, then he should be able to speak to all of us through the board."

"I think we should just g-go," Caleb said, looking around nervously.

"Everybody sit in a circle facing each other."

They sat cross-legged in a circle, with the edge of the board in each other's lap and their fingers resting gently on the plastic planchette.

"Okay, what do we do now?" Helen asked.

"We ask Gren to show up and answer some questions. The little arrow thing will move by itself, or it should, when we ask the questions."

Caleb was getting angry that Scares wasn't taking this seriously, or was it Gren who was getting mad?

"So, Mr. Gren, are you a ghost or demon? Just what are you?"

A strong breeze whipped through the trees and glided across the flowing brook. The feeling was electric.

The planchette started to go crazy as it began to spell: -I-W-A-N-T-

"Are you moving it?" Scares asked.

"No, are you?"

It continued: -A-

"This is freaking me out so bad," Scares said. "Are you doing this, little guy?"

"No, h-he is. Gren is."

Caleb's head started moving up and down erratically as his pupils disappeared.

-B-O-D-Y

"Hey, are you okay?" Helen yelled and touched his shoulder.

"What the fuck is wrong with him?" Scares asked. "What wants a body? This Tulpa thing?"

"This happened to him at the pizza place. Caleb, wake up!"

"Let's just go!" Scares said, grabbing Helen and helping her to her feet.

"No, I'm not leaving him here."

Caleb opened his eyes and took a loud gasp.

"You scared the hell out of me. Are you okay?" Helen asked, her eyes filled with tears.

"I'm g-gonna build him a b-body."

Scares and Helen looked at each other.

"Okay, I think it's time to go," Scares said.

"Is Scares scared?" Helen teased.

The scarecrow-thin boy puffed up. "No, of course not. I actually think this really is pretty damn cool. I mean, I know a kid who talks to sentient imaginary friends in the woods."

"This is not the same way we came," Helen said.

"We are headed the right way," Scares said.

"What's that smell?"

"Aw, I don't know," Scares said, putting his hand up to his face.

Helen stopped walking, her eyes wide. "Jesus … is that?"

"A dead person."

Propped under the tree was Deputy Dwight Greer. His head had been bashed in.

Scares started retching.

Helen bent down and read the name badge. "Greer."

Caleb smiled.

35

Scares stole glances at Helen as they chugged down the dirt road in his van, leaving the forest in their rear view.

"What the hell was that?" Scares asked, voice trembling. "I know that guy from around town. Who would kill a deputy?"

"Calm down." Helen turned to look at Caleb.

"What if that *thing* … Tulpa, did this?"

"Caleb, what is Gren, really?"

"Like I told you, he is my T-Tulpa. I learned how to m-make him on the internet."

"This is like a Slender Man thing, right? Scares said.

"What's a Slender Man thing?" Helen asked.

"Some ten-year-old girls created this shadow man from their imagination a few years back. They learned how to do it on the internet. It started as make-believe, but they said it became real. It fucking told them to kill a neighbor girl with a butcher knife."

"What happened?"

"The two little girls invited their neighbor over to play, and they stabbed her to death," Scares said, nearly hyperventilating at the thought that he had just seen something truly supernatural. "I think you summoned a demon, man! A goddamned demon!"

"That's crazy! I need a cigarette." Helen opened up the glove box and started going through its contents.

"Hey, close that!" Scares said, shaking his head in panic.

She took out a bottle of cheap cologne and a pair of bright pink panties. "Uh-huh, I'd like to present Exhibit A to the jury. What am I looking for again?"

Scares awkwardly tried to grab the panties from her hand, but Helen was too quick and pulled them away.

"That is not for your eyes! Give me!"

"Do you have a habit of stealing ladies' undies?

"No!" he said, going back and forth, trying to take them from her. "These belong to a girl I used to date at the video store!"

"Okay … calm down," she said as he snatched them from her hand.

Helen continued to dig in the glove box and pulled out a pistol. "Is this real?"

Scares held up his hand. "Whoa, be careful; it's loaded."

"What the hell are you doing with a gun?" She rolled her eyes and held the gun away from her like it was going to go off.

"Protection."

"Protection from what?"

"Those assholes at school," he said, reaching over to take the gun. "They used to come at me pretty bad, so I got it to …"

"What, to shoot them?" She asked, placing it back in the glove box and slamming it shut.

"You don't understand what it's like to be bullied every day. You're cool and beautiful. Fuck those assholes!"

"You don't need a gun. You just need …"

Scares looked at her.

"Friends. I've got your back."

Scares relaxed a bit as they shared a moment.

"You think I'm beautiful?"

He leaned in to kiss Helen but Caleb kicked the back of his seat, causing Scares to weave into the other lane.

"Look out!" Helen yelled.

A mail truck was coming around the curve.

Scares jerked the wheel, but the van hydroplaned and spun around before coming to a jolting standstill in the ditch.

"Helen! Are you okay?" Scares asked.

"I'm okay, I think," she said, touching her head. "Ouch."

"I'm going to call an ambulance," Scares said.

"No, I'm fine. My dad would kill me."

"Wait, how's Caleb?" Helen asked.

Scares looked in the backseat. The side door of the van was open.

"He's gone?"

A police cruiser happened to be driving by and stopped. The window came down to reveal Sheriff Darter. "Helen? Are you okay?"

"Thank God! We just saw a dead body in the woods. I think it was a policeman … a deputy." Helen said.

The Sheriff smirked. "Damn, you kids playing a joke on me?"

"What? No."

"I got a chain in the trunk. Let me back my car up to your bumper."

The Sheriff's car backed up.

“I don’t think he believes us. Should we tell him Caleb was with us?” Helen said.

“No, we’ll go and look for him ourselves.”

Sheriff Darter backed his car up and got out. “The weather is only supposed to get nastier these next few days, so only be out if you have to be. Now, let me get the chain and get you two back on the road,” he said as he lifted the lid of the trunk and happily whistled a tune.

“Aren’t you gonna call in what we told you?” Helen said.

“Oh, I did. Local police and more deputies are on their way.”

“I don’t hear any sirens.” Scares said.

“Don’t worry, They are on the way. Are you two okay?”

“Yeah, we’re fine. Thank you.”

“My pleasure, angel. Now take this chain and hook it around your bumper,” he told Scares, throwing him the chain.

Helen glanced in the trunk and noticed a lot of odd junk for a policeman to be carrying around.

“Okay, I got it on,” Scares said with a thumbs up.

The sheriff slammed the trunk, which caused Helen to jump. “I can’t see to back up with the trunk open.”

Helen stood to the side as her granddad pulled the van back onto the road.

After removing the chains, the sheriff pulled up beside the van on Helen’s side and leaned his head out the window. “Now, you two should probably head on home.”

Helen nodded her head. “Good idea.”

Sheriff Darter tipped his hat and drove off.

“That was a little weird, huh?” Scares said.

Helen shook her head. “Super weird.”

36

From *Ancient Voices Within Us All: A Study of Tulpamancery* by Doctor Barry Tenzin Dorjee, PhD, page 73:

Western interpreters and occultists of the Tibetan Buddhist disciplines, such as the French explorer Alexandra David-Neel (1868-1969), describe how she experimented with making a Tulpa in the form of a 'Jolly Monk' while visiting a secluded Buddhist temple in the mountains of Tibet. Her account states that others observed the self-described *Mind Monster*, not just herself, and she told of how it became more sinister under the guise of protecting her from others. It was self-motivated and dangerous, growing in power the longer it drew energy. As time went on, she was forced to dissolve it. She claims it did not go peacefully and put up a fight that nearly killed her companion. This is the power of the human mind.

Tulpas are not to be confused with Dissociative Identity Disorder (DID) and other specified Dissociative Disorders (OSDD-1s), which are post-traumatic mental disorders that cause pathological multiplicity. Although, it's not unusual for those conditions to be mistaken as experiencing something non-pathological, such as demonic possession or imaginary friends, or even Tulpas. The distinction between the pathological and the phenomenon of Tulpamancery lies in the patients' telekinetic abilities and that they are intentionally created. They are pulled into awareness.

I met with Caleb Jenkins under the assumption that what he was experiencing was solely a psychiatric phenomenon, a coping mechanism to deal with the murder of his mother, but I also had a hunch after our first session that he had somehow formed a powerful Tulpa, and it was fighting to become sentient. I had hoped that the case of Mr. Mopsey, and the young mother convicted of killing her husband, was one of a kind. Caleb was going down the same path, and no one around him was safe. I had to stop this, and to stop it I needed to speak with the young girl who created Mopsey. I asked a close friend from college to meet with me. She ended up being the mother's attorney and has access to the girl Bethany Ann Laemmle who was in state care.

37

Bill Hall thought he heard a child screaming among the rusted machines. It was already late in the evening, and the sun had turned the brown field a fiery orange. The bloodcurdling wail started right after the old combine engine rattled to life.

The old farmer was sitting on his front porch running the blade of his pocketknife across a whetstone when he heard the old engine crank up. That was an odd sound considering that particular engine hadn't been started in over twenty years. He put away his knife and started out toward the field.

The noise also made its way to Lois, who was busy hanging clothes on a line in the side yard. She called out to her husband, who was preparing his next sermon in his study.

They both rushed across the field to the source of the sound. Someone was in the driver's seat of the rusted Massy Ferguson harvester. Its massive thresher was whirling and sprayed blood in all directions painting the grass a shiny, wet red.

Bill thought for sure the machine's spinning teeth had caught the boy. The old farmer climbed up the side of the roaring machine and switched the key off. The spinning red blades came to a halt as the old engine thumped one last time before the combine went back to sleep.

It wasn't until Bill climbed back down that he noticed the bright yellow rooster key chain held tight in his hand. It dawned on him what exactly that meant, the impossibility of it being there. "That just can't be."

"What happened? Was that Caleb screaming?" An out of breath Lois asked as she ran up on the bloody scene, with Nestor running up just behind her.

"Bill?" Lois yelled, trying to break the farmer out of his stunned expression.

"I … I don't know. Ole Gruff is over there, or what's left of him," he said, pointing to the severed head of the goat, tossed just twenty feet from the front left tire of the tractor. Strings of bloody meat hung from its neck, and other pieces of its body lay strewn across the dead grass. A lone hoofed leg dangled inside the gore-soaked thresher of the machine.

"Oh, God … Caleb!" Lois blurted out when she spotted Caleb.

"I'll go back to the house and call an ambulance," Nestor said and started back in a steady trot.

"I don't understand," Bill said. His eyes wide, and his jaw dropped.

Caleb was standing just around the front of the machine.

"Thank God!" Lois said, with heavy breaths, as she took Caleb into her arms. She searched his body for any wounds.

"Are you hurt?"

Caleb kept his gaze focused on the dead goat.

A red-faced Nestor ran back. "The ambulance is on its way. Is Caleb okay?"

"It was just the goat," Lois said.

"Why did you do that to the goat, boy?" Bill Hall asked. His large hands rested on his hips. His body straight and rigid.

"Mr. Hall asked you a question," Nestor said.

Caleb didn't move. His expression was blank. He was in shock.

"Where did you get these keys?" Bill asked, pointing at the tractor.

"The g-goat started to chase me, and I c-climbed up to stay safe."

"And these keys?" he said, shaking them.

"I p-put the keys in the ignition to try and s-scare the goat."

Bill lunged at the boy and grabbed him. "How did you get these goddamned keys?"

"L-let go!" Caleb yelled.

"He's just a boy." Lois said.

"Lois, let me handle this. Mr. Hall, you need to watch your language."

"Or what? It's a simple question, is all!" Bill roared.

Nestor backed down.

"We'll reimburse you for the goat," Lois answered, pushing Bill back with all she had. "Let him be!"

"Looks like your wife wears the pants in the family."

Nestor's face turned red.

"I want a goddamned answer as to how this boy got these keys."

"M-my friend gave them to me."

Bill whirled around. "Who's this friend? Is he out here somewhere?"

"Maybe he found the keys in the combine?" Nestor said.

"That's not possible."

"I'm taking Caleb home," Lois said.

"Who's this friend? Is he out here with you?" Bill asked, looking around.

Caleb shook his head. Tears welled in his eyes. Gren's voice told him not to tell the farmer about him or the woods.

"Then where?" Bill insisted. "I'm not going to let this go."

"He stays in the w-woods," Caleb said, pointing toward the trees.

Bill could see the sheriff's cruiser pull up with the ambulance.

"You call the sheriff, too?" Bill said.

"No, he must have heard the 911 call over the scanner," Nestor said.

"I hate the law," Bill said, kicking a dirt clod.

"Howdy, Bill, Lois … Nestor," Sheriff Darter said and tipped his hat.

"Marcus," Bill answered. "Hate to bother you over a dead goat."

Sheriff Darter pushed back his cowboy hat and nudged the severed goat's head with his boot. "Damn, Ole Gruff finally met his end. What happened?"

"The Jenkins's boy somehow started the combine, and the goat got caught in its thresher."

"My God, but the boy is okay?" Marcus asked. He took off his hat and walked over to Lois and placed his hand on her shoulder. "I heard the paramedics. Don't worry. We'll get him checked out. Accidents happen."

Lois glared at Bill. "That goat was a nuisance, anyway. He attacked Caleb, and others, on several occasions."

"Well, it wouldn't have happened if he hadn't been trespassing on my property," Bill snapped.

Sheriff Darter raised his hand to the irate farmer. "Okay, that's enough. We should just count our blessings that the boy wasn't hurt. I'm sure Nestor and Lois have no problem with paying you for the goat. Are we good here, Bill?" Marcus said while cutting Bill a sharp stare.

"Yeah, I reckon!"

Two paramedics approached and took Caleb to the side, but Lois pulled him back. "He's okay, just shaken up."

"Well, the paramedics should still take a look at him, just in case," Sheriff Darter said.

"Thanks for stopping by, Sheriff, but you can get off my property now," Bill said, pointing toward the road.

"That goat was ornery, kinda like his owner," Sheriff Darter said and stood looking up to the hulking farmer.

"You gonna find out just how ornery."

"That a threat, Bill?"

Bill grumbled under his breath.

"I can't believe that thing still starts. Are those the keys you said you lost all those years ago, Bill?" The sheriff asked.

Bill held up the yellow rooster key chain. "Yeah, this is them."

The sheriff's eyes widened, but he quickly regained his calm demeanor.

"I haven't had a bowl of cornflakes in a long time. Probably been twenty-five years. Well, I guess there's nothing else to be done here. Y'all have a good day now," the Sheriff said, tipping his hat and walking back to his squad car.

38

Hall Farm

2007

It was a tranquil spring day. The sky was an endless blue. Nina Hall was out hanging wash on the lines and humming the old gospel song "Bringing in the Sheaves". Her husband, Bill, had not been lying beside her when she woke up this morning, which she found strange. His pillow didn't have his familiar indent, so she knew that he hadn't even gone to bed last night.

Nina had just turned forty but still possessed the beauty that her farming husband had fallen in love with in high school, although her coal-black now had threads of silver.

She pinned the last of the large bedsheets on the cord and looked out over the field that stretched out for over twenty acres. Lying on the ground, just a few feet away, was a bright yellow rubber key chain in the shape of a rooster. She knew that was the key to her husband's combine tractor.

Nina walked over and grabbed the key, and when she stood back up with it, she spotted Bill walking into the old shed that sat just off from the main house.

"Bill?" she called out to him, but the wind was blowing, and he didn't hear her.

She walked to the weathered shed door and stopped just before opening it. Her husband was talking to someone. They were arguing, but she couldn't make out about what.

Nina opened the door a crack and saw Bill. He was covered in mud and holding a shovel. The other person was just out of sight.

"Bill, everything okay?" she said. "I found your keys to the harvester."

Her husband jerked around to face her. The other person went silent. "Good, I was looking for those."

"I'll just come in and give them to you."

Don't come in here!" he roared, which made her jump. He had never yelled at her like that. "Just go on up to the house. I'll be there in a minute to explain."

"You sure everything is alright?" she asked, pushing open the door wider, and that's when she saw the body of a girl. She looked like she was in her twenties with a thick mop of dark hair, and Nina recognized the pretty face as the girl she had seen in the newspaper. She was a Diamond Queen from a few years ago.

"I wish you had just done what I said," Bill said as he walked towards her, a shovel in his massive hands.

Nina screamed and started to run.

Bill chased her around the corner of the house, just in time to see her trip on the low wall of the old well that had been on the property since they moved there.

She attempted called out for her husband for help, but it came out as a pained whisper, and after a few moments the light darkened from someone standing over the opening.

"You should have listened to me and not come in," Bill said, before pulling a large sheet of tin over the hole.

39

It was noon on a Wednesday, and Dorjee was sipping tea, sitting at a bistro table outside Enlightenment on Third, his favorite café in German Town. The place was abnormally busy today. He marveled at how much Nashville had grown in the past few years. Parisian rattan chairs lined the patio beside small glass tables and vintage lighting hung outside and inside the small dining area. A white porcelain teapot rested on the two-person table where Barry sat.

He was waiting for his old girlfriend from college, who went off to Law School and become a sought-after criminal defense attorney. Elise Sloan was the entire package of looks and smarts, and not being with her was one of Barry's biggest regrets. They had met at USC and dated for a short time until they realized it just wasn't going to work. Her dream was to take the bar, and become a famous criminal lawyer, while he dreamed of exploring haunted houses and taking night courses on Tibetan mysticism. His classmates used to call him Doctor Strange in college.

Barry had arrived at the café early so he could people-watch. It was the one thing he loved to do when out. He would wait and watch like a patient hunter until he witnessed what he called *golden behavior*. It could be a weird mannerism, an odd quirk, or sometimes it was something more. He spied an Asian family having lunch a few tables over. The mother and father sat with a rigid posture, and the kids were well behaved. He was about to turn his attention away from the family when one of the boys took his cup and held it to the empty seat beside him as if giving a sip to someone only he could see. This resulted in the liquid pouring from the cup onto the seat.

"Hey, Strange," said the voice of a woman standing over him. Barry turned, but the light behind cast her in shadow. He raised a hand to block the sun and saw Elise's face.

"I haven't been called Dr. Strange since college," he said. She was as beautiful as he remembered. Memories came flooding back, and, for a second, he felt the old attraction to her.

Her smile was disarming as ever, and her long straight dark hair seemed made of silk. Barry stood to hug his old friend and former lover. "Wow, you haven't changed a bit. That smile is still a killer. Please, have a seat."

"Still the charmer, I see," Elise said, laying her purse on the table as she slid into the seat across from him.

"Tea? It's jasmine," he said.

"My favorite. You remembered."

Barry poured the tea. "It's super hot. A professional courtesy, of course," he said, but deep down, he hoped she had missed him as much as he had missed her.

He noticed the ring on her finger. "Oh, you got married. How did I miss that?"

"I'm in the middle of a divorce."

"Oh, I'm sorry to hear that, but you still wear the ring?" he said, trying to think of something witty to change the channel of the now awkwardness and, at the same time, trying not to smile. "You know what you get when you cross an elephant with a zebra?"

"Oh, still telling bad jokes, I see."

"Come on, what do you get?"

"I have no idea, but I'm sure you'll tell me," she said, with a flirty smile that would melt steel.

"Elephant zebra sin theta."

She buried her face in her hands. "Oh my god, that was terrible. A calculus joke?"

"Come on, they always kill at parties."

"Kill the mood, maybe. You haven't changed a bit, I swear. You are still the most lovable dork in the room," she said, taking a sip of tea.

"I read that you are representing Bethany Ann Laemmle's mother, Susan Laemmle?"

"Yes, I managed to get her a retrial for the murder of her husband, but only if I can convince a jury that her daughter's other personality did it."

Dr. Dorjee settled into his chair, and his tone grew more serious. "But it wasn't a split personality; it was a Tulpa."

"Bethany Ann Laemmle was mentally troubled due to horrific abuse perpetrated by her sick father, and her personality split to cope with it, and I believe that personality took over and pushed her father down those steps," Elsie said.

"But that still holds her responsible for killing her father."

"And you, once again, want to try and prove this Tulpa theory? Bethany will never get out of the psychiatric hospital, but at least proving she had a split will maybe keep her out of a psychiatric prison." Elise took an angry sip of her drink and cut him a hard look. A look he knew all too well.

"But in the process, I would condemn an innocent girl to a life in a mental ward. What if I could convince the jury that Bethany's Tulpa did kill her father?"

She laughed. "How the hell would you do that? Bring in an exorcist?"

"I'm not sure yet, but I'm getting closer to real proof."

"Tell you what, I'll make a deal with you. I've read your book, and in it, you say that a person's Tulpa can move things, sometimes even manifest, right?"

Barry nodded. "It has been reported."

"The trial is in two weeks. If you can get me video proof – enough proof that you win me over—I'll let you go with the Tulpa defense."

"I'll need access to her."

"I can make that happen. But if you can't convince me by two weeks, I'll need you to support my theory that Bethany Ann has Dissociative Identity Disorder, and we make a deal with the state."

Barry sat back and sighed. "It would contradict everything I said as an expert witness at her mother's first trial. It would go against all of my writings."

"Yes, but it will release an innocent woman. As you know, Bethany's mother is doing life for a crime that her daughter committed. What's more important: a little bit of professional ridicule, which you get already, or the chance to free at least one of them?"

"I'll get your proof," he said and leaned in.

She didn't pull back.

"I believe Bethany is an omnikinetic, not unlike a young patient I am currently treating. You know that children in dire home circumstances sometimes turn to imaginary friends to cope with their trauma. Well, in the case of an omnikinetic, they literally manifest a separate being that is a sentient living thing. I call children with this ability *Tulpamancers*. These mental constructs take yogis years of meditation and concentration, but these Tulpamancers can do it in mere months."

"Oh god, Barry. You still believe in ghosts and goblins?" she said and rolled her eyes. "I need a real expert witness, not a hunter of the supernatural. Maybe, you should become a ghost hunter? You were the leader in the field of imaginary companions, and you are a brilliant man, but this is the kind of shit that caused us to break up."

"It's true, sixty-five percent of all children have make-believe friends at some time in their lives. I have studied hundreds of them, but I have also encountered another phenomenon that solidifies a theory in the book that I am currently writing. He is so strong in his ability that he manifested a phantom bird in my office."

"You're kidding," she said, almost taking the hook, but she quickly shook her head and laughed at herself.

"No," he insisted.

Elise pushed herself back from the table and crossed her arms.

"This reminds me of a story my Jewish grandfather used to tell me when I was a little girl. You know I'm half-Jewish on my mother's side, which makes me Jewish. He used to tell me a story called *The Clay Boy*. It's about an older couple whose only child died. One day, a local village mystic overhears the woman lamenting about her dead boy. The mystic tells her how to make a new son out of clay.

"The grieving mother enacts the spell exactly as the mystic taught her. She digs a fresh lump of clay from the riverbank and cuts her palm to pour three drops of blood onto it. She sculpts a boy out of clay and dries him by the hearth."

Barry interrupted her. "I've heard a version of this, remember, I'm Doctor Strange. The boy comes to life, and at first, the couple is delighted. They treat him like a real son, but he does not stop growing and eats everything in the house. Then he goes into the field and eats their livestock, and then the boy eats his parents. The clay boy tears through the village, destroying everything in his path. It's a parable for letting grief and hate take over your life."

"That's pretty much it."

"I need to talk to Bethany's Tulpa so I can figure out how to stop the progression."

"Reality confusion is a precursor to borderline personality disorder. I'm sure you know that. I still think my girl has a textbook mental disorder that stems from physical and emotional abuse."

"Do you want me to work on this or not? I'm not crazy."

'Look, If you can prove that a Tulpa created by this girl's trauma killed her father—just like what you claim is happening with this new patient of yours—if you can make a viable connection, Bethany could move on, and so could her mother."

"Okay, where is she?"

"At the Medo Wellness Center, here. I'll send you the details and necessary paperwork." Elise gathered her purse and stood to leave.

"She's in Nashville? It was good seeing you," Barry said, standing as well.

They hugged.

"I'll text you the info when I have it," she said and turned to walk away.

"Wait, I have another joke for you," he said, waving his arms.

She stopped and smiled. “I don’t have time for a joke, Barry.”

“Knock, knock.”

“God, really?” She rolled her eyes.

“Come on, knock, knock.”

“Who’s there?”

“Sorry.”

“Sorry, who?”

“Sorry wrong door,” he said, but he wasn’t smiling.

“It didn’t use to be,” she said and walked away.

40

Tina Rathburn was driving way too fast to her blind date. She had never been one to go on blind dates, but a girlfriend of hers had been going on and on about a guy she worked with and thought he was Tina's perfect match. Tina hadn't been on a date in a while, not since she had started subbing at the Middle School. She was driving fast to the Chili's at Exit 25 just off the forty Interstate. It was a notorious speed trap, but Tina didn't want to be late. She hadn't been on a good date in months and was running late as usual. Her friends frequently said she would be late for her own funeral.

As she neared the exit, she saw blue lights in her rearview. The rain was pouring down again, and visibility was terrible. She pulled over as the blue lights settled behind her through the torrents of rainwater on her rearview mirror.

The nervous ex-beauty queen fixed her hair and touched up her makeup as a figure exited the vehicle and approached. She planned to use all of her feminine wiles to get out of this ticket. She could see in her rearview mirror the tall figure wore a wide-brimmed cowboy and a rain slicker, but then caught a glimpse of the type of vehicle that the person had exited from. It looked more like a normal truck than a police cruiser, which she thought was odd, but maybe it was another type of official police vehicle.

Tina was startled at a sudden tap at her window. She lowered the window and offered the sexiest smile she could muster. "I'm so sorry, officer, was I speeding?"

The man had his head lowered, and the brim of his hat covered the top of his face. The rain was coming down like bullets.

"License and registration," the man said in a low southern drawl.

"Oh, I have it right here. You might know me; I'm Tina Rathburn. You must be new, I work at Wheeler Middle School."

Silence.

"I was a Wheeler Diamond Queen. I've done a lot of work for the community over the past three years."

The man's head remained lowered.

"Do you need anything else? Aren't you normally in a police car?" she asked suspiciously.

"Wait here. Turn off your engine," he said and walked to the back of her car.

"Can I keep listening to the radio? Hello?" she asked, but he had already disappeared into the downpour.

She turned the Internet radio to an old Hank Williams country song but kept scrolling until she landed on an upbeat pop song. She started to sing along badly while glancing in the mirror to keep an eye on the officer.

"Come on," she whined as she looked back again, but now her breath was fogging the windows, so she could no longer see the man.

She waited for a few more minutes until there was a slight break in the downpour. She opened the door and leaned out to see if she could get a glimpse of the policeman. "Hello? I kinda need to get going. Is everything okay?" she said but heard no reply and saw no sign of the man.

Tina craned her head further and noticed the officer was arguing with a second man, who was dressed in plain clothes. It didn't take long until the confrontation turned physical. One pushed the other down, and she lost sight of both men. She slammed the door shut and rifled through her purse for her cell phone, but in the panic forgot to lock her door.

"Keep it together, Tina," she said, turning her purse over and dumping its contents on the seat. Her phone was the last thing to fall out, and it slipped between the seats.

"Are you kidding me?!" She glanced out the windows before sticking her hand under the seat. She managed to touch the edge of her phone with her fingertips but couldn't quite grab it.

The rain came down harder.

She gave up on her current strategy and swung her upper body into the backseat to get a better angle on her phone. That's when she remembered that she had forgotten to lock the doors.

Her whole body tensed as she heard the door open behind her.

"Hello?" she said.

An electrical cord gently looped over her head and pinched tight. It felt like a boa constrictor around her neck as the man lifted Tina out of the car. The kicking and fighting were brief, and the man dragged her limp body off into the flood.

41

Caleb was cutting through the woods with his glove and new bat in his hands. The strong breeze nearly blew him down at one point. He could hear the water splashing and bubbling in the small creek that ran through the heart of the woods. He was excited to keep working on his most recent and most impressive sculpture, one that he had been working on every day after school for a month—a life-sized boy made of clay. It was the most perfect thing he had ever sculpted, and it looked like a real thirteen-year-old boy, down to the smallest detail.

He had made a lot of progress over the past few weeks. The life-sized sculpture now had legs and a torso. The head sat on the bank near the water's edge, and Caleb bent over and picked up the detailed face, holding it just inches away from his face. It was a little weathered from being outside, and it's lips were turned downward into a frown.

"I don't remember making you look so unhappy," he said, attempting to fix the smile. He placed the head onto the body and took a step back to admire his work. "There, now you have a body just like you asked for."

Caleb noticed someone on the other side of the stream. As the person moved closer, he could see it was Bill Hall.

"Caleb, that you?"

Caleb hid behind a tree.

"Wait, I'm not mad about the goat. I just wanted to talk to your friend for a minute. Is that him? I can't see very well?" Bill shouted as he pulled a pocket knife from his overalls and waved it in front of his barrel chest. "I just want to ask him how he got those keys!"

Caleb tried to control his breathing, but his chest was wheezing.

"You don't have to be scared of me!"

Caleb could hear the farmer splattering through the water.

"I remember coming here to swim when I was about your age. It felt so good after a long hot day of baling hay," he said, trying to sound friendly. He stepped from the water and approached the clay sculpture from behind, thinking it was Caleb.

"Hey," Bill said and touched the shoulder of the sculpture, but pulled his hand back. It took a moment to register that it was made of clay. "You got talent; I will give you that."

Caleb coughed.

Bill's head turned sharply.

"Oh, are we playing hide and seek?" he said, moving toward Caleb. "I'm good at that game."

Caleb picked up his baseball bat, gripping it with both hands as Bill got closer and closer.

Caleb bolted away from Bill.

"Oh, you wanna play, do ya?" he yelled, lunging at Caleb.

"You're not going to hurt *us*!"

"What you talking about? What you think you're gonna do with that bat, boy?"

Caleb swung it, but the big farmer easily caught it.

The scared boy let go and sprinted toward home.

"Hold up! I don't want to hurt you! I just need to talk to your friend about those keys!"

After Caleb had disappeared, Bill sat down on a rock and started cussing and whining.

"You're pathetic," a male voice said from behind.

Bill knew the voice. "You following me now? The boy knows about my wife being in the well, somehow. I think he knows about those girls, too. We should just leave Wheeler's Cove."

"There's no leaving, ever," the voice said as he wrapped a cord around Bill's neck and pulled it tight.

42

Sheriff Marcus Darter's police interceptor pulled down the long gravel driveway and up to the side of Lois and Nestor Jenkins's house. The afternoon sun was still hanging in the cloudless sky.

The sheriff got out and stretched. "Damn, I'm getting too old for this shit."

Lois was walking in from the clothesline with a basket full of clean linens.

"Sheriff, what brings you out?"

"I sure do love the smell of fresh, clean laundry. A glass of your iced tea would have been enough of a reason."

Nestor stepped onto the front porch with his bible in one hand and his reading glasses in the other. "Sheriff."

"Hate to bother you folks," he said, with his customary old-school hat tip. "I wanted to check on Caleb. Also, to deliver some bad news: we found your neighbor, Bill Hall, dead in the woods."

"He's dead? How?"

"Looks like he took a fall into the creek and drowned."

"My God," Lois said, placing her hand on her heart.

"When did it happen?" Nestor asked. He leaned back and rubbed his brow as if he had a terrible headache.

"A few hours ago. We know Caleb plays in those woods and said something about a friend who lives out there? I need to ask Caleb if he saw anything."

"He's not here right now, but he should be back anytime."

"Let me get my keys, and I'll help you look for Caleb," Nestor said.

"No need, Nestor. I think it would be better if you stayed here and gave me a call when he comes back. What part of the woods does he like to play in the most?"

"By the stream. He gets clay from the bank to use for his sculptures."

"That's right near where we found Bill's body."

"Is Caleb in danger?" Lois asked.

"I don't think so, but I'm headed back to the woods to have a look. You folks give us a call when Caleb comes home, and dispatch will let me know. Like I said, sorry to bother you."

The sheriff tipped his cowboy hat again.

"Okay, will do. Thanks, Marcus!" Nestor said.

As Sheriff Darter walked back to the squad car, he heard a loud banging from inside his trunk. He turned back to the porch to see if Nestor and Lois had heard it too, but they were still smiling and waving.

"Damn car has been acting up! We'll get this sorted out." He walked to the back of the car and the banging stopped.

43

It was early morning when Dorjee pulled up to the Medo Center of Wellness. The building was a modern glass structure, and Dorjee's bright green Prius stood out among the larger cars and vans parked there. He scanned the deserted entry and saw the valet walking up to open his door. "My Porsche is in the shop," Barry joked, but the grumpy attendant wasn't in the mood for jokes.

The front doors opened into a lush inner courtyard. Patients walked around, listening to earbuds or reading books. A few burly men dressed in white watched over the yard. Barry had been to Medo years ago right after college to intern, but had no idea that Bethany had been transferred here.

The husky lady at the front desk was yelling at an orderly; she did a double take on seeing Barry. She was rosy-cheeked and built like someone who lifted heavy things—and people—all day. He lowered his head, hoping to go unnoticed by the overzealous nurse, but it didn't work.

"Oh, my Lord in Heaven, if it isn't that cutie, Dr. Barry Dorjee!" she called as she moved around the large front desk to embrace the doctor.

"You still have the strongest bear hug I've ever felt," Barry sighed as she squeezed the breath from his body.

"It's good to see my favorite little country Buddhist. Where have you been? You look like you've put on some weight. You know I like a man with a little meat on his bones. We never got that drink together."

"I don't drink, remember?" he said, struggling to break her hold.

"You can watch me drink, and I'll just watch you looking fine."

"Tempting, but I'm here for work."

"What kind of work, sweet cheeks?"

"To interview the Laemmle girl."

Her face lost its rosy smile.

"That girl scares the hell out of me."

"Why?"

"I've seen things that will make you question what's real or not. I started wearing this around my neck on the nights when I make my rounds," she said, showing Barry a silver cross around her neck.

"That girl is evil."

"I'm here on behalf of her attorney. She and Bethany's mother are going back to trial."

"If the mom didn't kill her husband, who did?"

"Bethany turns eighteen tomorrow," Barry said, giving the nurse a significant look.

"Of course," she said. "Sit down over there and give me a minute to make a phone call to confirm, not that I don't trust your sexy little face."

Barry smiled but frowned when she turned her back. This woman was something else. He sat near an old vending machine and looked over its contents.

Down the hall, he could swear he heard something that sounded like birds fluttering their wings.

For the first few years after moving to Tennessee, his mother had rented a small house in Leipers Fork in Williamson. Barry was in the fourth grade and was the only brown-skinned boy at the school. His first years in a new place and new culture were rough. He remembered fighting a lot back then and keeping to himself. His only friend was a little girl named Hallie. They had met on the playground near the swing set right before summer break, and they soon became fast friends. There were always a host of sparrows in the trees around the playground. The memory of her had been foggy for years, but it came back the day he met Caleb.

The two friends became inseparable, and they played every day of that beautiful summer like it was never going to end. One day, Barry went to meet her at their tree, and she wasn't there, and the birds were gone, except for a single dead sparrow laying near the swings. He looked for Hallie everywhere, but he couldn't do anything else.

"I see you out here every day looking for something," an inquisitive teacher asked. "Are you sad that they took down the swings?" he asked, pointing to where the swings had been. The teacher was one of Barry's favorites, a younger and cooler teacher than most.

"No, I'm looking for my best friend, but I think she moved away," Barry replied, his face sad, as his eyes darted back and forth across the spot where he usually found Hallie waiting.

"What's her name? Maybe I can help you find her."

"Hallie."

The teacher looked like someone had punched him in the stomach.

"Mr. Klein, what's wrong?" Barry asked, seeing the confusion on the teacher's face.

"How do you know that name?"

"She told me," he said.

"What does she look like, your friend?"

"She's pretty. She has blonde hair in pigtails and wears a—"

"Purple dress with little white dots all over it?"

"Yeah, she always wore that. You know her?"

"That was my daughter's favorite dress. It's the one we buried her in and the one I see when I imagine her. She's all I thought about for years. I can still hear her voice. She used to talk to me."

The sad, worn father had wanted his dead daughter back so badly that he had inadvertently created a Tulpa. In Greek mythology sparrows were considered a symbol of love, while in some cultures a seeing a dead sparrow was a symbol of change, transformation, and even death.

"Barry!" a female voice woke him from this day-mare. "I can take you to her room now, sweetie," the love-struck head nurse said.

"I'm going to take my phone in to record if that's okay?"

"Electronics act funny on this side of the building, and you usually need to make prior request, but I'll let you slide."

They walked to the end of a clean, shiny hallway and entered an older portion of the ward. The more modern block had been added in the nineties and gave the impression that the hospital was more than a place to lock away insane and dangerous patients. They continued down a long, dingy corridor, lined with steel-enforced doors, each with electronic security locks, until they stopped at Bethany's room.

"This is her," the nurse said. "Good luck."

She unlocked an electronic lock to the left of the door, opened it, and held it for Dorjee. "Go ahead. She's pretty calm once she's had her meds."

"Okay, thanks. I think I have it from here. I'm sure she'll remember me. I interviewed her during the first trial."

"Alright then, just hit that buzzer to reach the front desk. The door stays locked until you request me to open it."

"Same buzzer to request that?"

"Yep," she said and left the room in a hurry.

Dr. Dorjee looked around the large room. Thick shades covered the windows with only a hint of light peeking in. It took a few seconds for his eyes to adjust. Once they did, he could see hundreds, possibly thousands of intricate drawings pinned and taped to every inch of the room's four walls. He stepped closer and saw a drawing of a happy cartoon pig in a top hat. All of the pictures featured this smiling pig. Mr. Mopsey.

"I remember you," a youthful but solemn voice said from the shadows.

"Bethany?"

"That's right. It's Dr. Dorjee, right? Barry?"

"Yes. Why is it so cold in here? My teeth are chattering."

"Mopsey likes it cold, you know that."

He set up a tripod for his cell phone to record the interview. He was trembling. Bethany sat on the bed with her back turned away from him.

"What can I do for you?" Bethany asked in the normal, sweet voice of an eighteen-year-old girl. She turned slowly to face him, and her features didn't match her tone. The fluorescent light in the room made her appear sickly pale, haggard, and her eyes were sunken into her skull. She looked like someone whose life was draining away. The Tulpa was feeding on her.

"I am here to talk to you about your mother … and you."

"*Dorjee, Dor-jee, that's a real funny name*!" a new voice cut in. This voice sounded like an upbeat cartoon character.

"Bethany?"

"Let me guess, Dor-jee head. You are here to help get Bethany's bitch mother released from prison. She never protected Bethany, and she's right where she deserves to be, and Bethany is with me! Snort! Snort! Best friends … forever!"

Barry fumbled with the button on his phone's camera to start recording. "Who am I speaking with?"

"*Who do you think*?"

"Mopsey?"

"Bingo! *Snort! Snort! I was Bethany's only friend—her best friend. She's not lonely anymore. Not forever, cause Mopsey is here to save the day!*"

"You've taken complete control of her body since she was brought here? I thought you lived inside the doll and just spoke with her?"

"*I thought you were smart, Dor-jee? I have been in control of Bethany's body since the day I pushed her father down the stairs. She asked me to take over and protect her. I fixed that problem, real good!*"

"Bethany brought you to life, and this is how you repay her?"

"*We all start from nothing and become something. That sounds fair to me, Dor-jee! Snort!*"

"I need you to leave."

"*You would like that, wouldn't you? Wouldn't you, ole Dorjee-borjee? Snort!*"

"Bethany deserves to exist too. You don't have the right to take someone's body and do what you wish."

"Her father was doing terrible things to her. I'm her hero!"

Bethany stood and started jumping up and down on her bed.

"*Mopsey the pig wants you to always be truthful and never to lie! Mopsey the pig wants to be friends way, way up in the sky! Mopsey the pig says you better fly! Cause Mopsey is gonna eat both of your eyes! Snort!*"

Barry gripped the side of his chair, fighting the urge to get up and run from the room. "How do I know you're not just a split personality that Bethany created to cope with her father's abuse?"

Bethany stopped jumping, and her smiling face became hard. *"I am not imaginary. I am real!"*

"Prove it," Barry said with crossed arms.

"You want me to show you how I really look?"

Dr. Dorjee nodded. "You're too scared."

Bethany grabbed a stuffed animal off the nightstand and turned her back on Barry to get on all fours. Her body contorted, and as she arched her back and snorted, she whirled around to show her eyes had changed to black. Behind her on the wall was a giant shadow that looked like the head of a pig. She was holding the stuffed animal out in front of her, which Barry now saw was a stuffed Mopsey. Its head was moving from side to side.

"Snort! Snort! Do you see, Dorjee-borjee?"

The doctor let out a gasp but composed himself and continued the interview. "What is that?"

"It made her feel safe. She confided in it so much that I was born. There is only the real Mopsey now."

"You say you love Bethany and want her to be safe, then enter the doll and give back her body."

"No!"

"Then you don't love Bethany?"

Bethany looked confused and backed away. *"You're trying to trick me, Dorjee Dorky Head, but you can't. Snort!"*

"No, you said that you cared and loved her, so prove it. To me, you're just an imaginary cartoon character. Mopsey isn't real. I'm talking to a girl named Bethany right now, who made you up."

"Snort! Snort! Shut up, you fucking asshole!"

'Help … me," Bethany screamed, putting her hands to her face, and collapsing onto the bed.

"Bethany?" Dr. Dorjee asked as he rushed over. He grabbed the stuffed Mopsey and threw it in the corner.

She rose to show tear-filled eyes. "What happened? Where am I?"

"You're inside a room at the Medo Psychiatric Hospital in Nashville, Tennessee."

"How did I get here? Where's my mama?"

"You were brought here after Mopsey pushed your father down the stairs."

"How long have I been here?"

"Six years."

"Six?" she asked. Bethany looked at her hands, felt her hair, and then started screaming.

"How old do you think you are?" Barry asked, trying to calm her.

"I just turned twelve," she said. "But I know I'm not. It's hard to explain, but it's like I've been an imaginary little girl in Mopsey's mind all this time."

"What's the last thing you remember?"

"I was in my bedroom talking to Mopsey. I asked him to . . ." she started to cry. "My father was walking up the stairs, and Mopsey told me to hide in the closet. I heard a loud noise. Then the police came into my room and took me away. They covered my head with a jacket, and then I was in a dark place, until now."

"I'm a psychiatric doctor trying to help you and your mother, and I . . ."

He heard a noise from the corner. Bethany jumped into Barry's arm, hugging tight. "Don't say his name. Try not to think about him. That gives him strength."

"Stay here," the doctor said as he cautiously slid off the bed and walked around its edge to the source of the sound.

"Oh, damn," he whispered when he realized Mopsey had vanished. He walked back to where he was sitting and scanned the entirety of the polished floor. Then he noticed the stuffed animal's bright pink tail hanging out from under the bed.

The lights flickered.

Barry moved slowly to the end of the bed as the fluffy pink tail disappeared underneath. Fear crept up his spine, and he broke into a cold sweat. He slowly dropped to the ground to look, but there was nothing under the bed.

Bethany screamed again.

Dr. Dorjee jumped up to see the stuffed toy sitting in Bethany's lap. He quickly grabbed Mopsey and went to rip its head off.

"No! Don't do that!"

The doctor stopped. "Why? I'm going to destroy it."

Bethany wiped the tears away and held out her hands. "No, that won't work. Hand him to me. We shared each other's thoughts for years. I created him, so I'm the only one that can destroy him."

Dr. Dorjee reluctantly handed the stuffed animal to the girl. "You're sure about this?"

"Yes," she said and looked into the toy's eyes. Its black eyes reflected her own blue eyes. "I don't want to be friends with you anymore! You are not real!" Bethany shouted over and over as she pictured Mopsey in her mind's eye, slowly dissolving into smoke and floating away. Bethany said it again and again, and the last time she screamed it as she ripped the doll's head off.

She grew limp and slumped over.

"Bethany Ann? Bethany Ann!" Dr. Dorjee yelled and felt her neck for a pulse, but there was none. He started to do CPR as orderlies poured into the room.

"What happened?" A tall, dark-skinned orderly asked.

"She just stopped breathing," he said, moving away from the bed as they worked to revive the unconscious Bethany Ann.

"Please leave the room, sir."

"Is she going to be alright?" Barry asked. He was in shock, obsessively running his fingers through his hair. His cell phone rang, which made him jump. He stepped into the hall. "Hello, this is Dr. Barry Tenzin Dorjee."

"This is Lois Jenkins. Are you okay? You sound funny."

"I'm doing ... fine. How are you, Mrs. Jenkins?"

"It's Caleb."

"What about him?"

"He's ... missing, and the police found our neighbor dead in the woods where Caleb plays."

"Are you sure he's missing? Maybe, he's just out playing."

"The sheriff just stopped by looking for him."

The orderly walked into the hall. Her face was blank.

"How is Bethany?"

"She... didn't make it."

Dorjee saw spots, and his head spun as he stumbled down the hall.

"Doctor?" Lois's voice asked on the other end of the phone.

He slowly put the phone back to his ear. His heart was beating out of his chest.

"Hello?" she asked again.

"I can be at your house within the hour. I'm afraid that Caleb is in terrible danger. If he comes home, keep him there until I arrive."

44

Scares drove the van fast down the dirt road beside the woods, with Helen in the passenger seat beside him.

"You called Caleb's aunt, right? What did you say?" Scares said.

"That Caleb was missing, and I said I'd look for him. I mean that *we* would go looking for him, well until my cell reception went away. I haven't had a bar in a while. Thanks for doing this."

"Hey, is that the sheriff's car?" Scares said and pointed to the patrol car parked off the road.

Scares whipped the van right up to the back of the car, and both of them got out.

"Did you hear something?" Helen asked.

"I definitely heard something."

"It sounded like screaming, and it was coming from the trunk."

Scares looked over at Helen in disbelief.

"Is someone in the Sheriff's trunk?"

"We need to open it."

"I've got a crowbar," he said and dashed back to the van.

Helen touched the top of the closed trunk just as a loud bang came from the inside. She jerked back and then lowered her head to the lock.

"Hello, who's in there? Hey, Scares, hurry up!"

Scares searched his van and finally came up with a crowbar.

"Got it!"

A rock suddenly crashed into the center of the van's windshield.

"What the fuck?" Scares said as he looked back toward the edge of the trees.

Laughing

"Who's there?"

"Look who it is, my second favorite little psycho," a voice said.

Scares knew that voice well.

Mark Mallory and Eric Frame walked out of the woods. They were both laughing, and Mark held a long stick. "You hitting that new girl? Damn, I'm impressed. I always thought you were a fag. You impressed, Eric?"

"Absolutely."

"Get the fuck outta here, Mallory. This isn't the time. You see that police car over there?" Scares said, his hands up like he was ready to fight, but at the same time was making his way back to the van's open passenger door.

"We could use your help," Helen said as she walked up to the potential confrontation.

"Oh, you can help this out," Mark said and grabbed his crotch.

"You need to leave," Scares said, pulling a pistol from his glove box.

"Shit, he's got a gun," Eric said.

"Scares, they aren't worth it," Helen said. She could see that his hands were shaking more from rage than nerves.

"These assholes have messed with me since fourth grade! I've got the power now, bitches," Scares said, his voice trembling as he moved the barrel of the gun from one Hyena to the other.

"Dude, Mark made me come with him. I didn't want to do—"

"Shut up, Eric," Mark said. "I know I've been pretty hard on you over the years, but I was dealing with a lot at home. I want to change. This made me realize that I've gone too far." He gave Scares a sincere look with his hands held up.

Helen noticed he was moving closer to Scares. "Look out!"

Mark swung the stick he was holding and hit Scares in the wrist. The gun went flying and landed at Eric's feet.

"Hand it to me!" Mark yelled.

"I think we should just go, man," Eric said.

Mark snatched the gun out of his hand and pointed it at Helen and Scares. "You dumbass. You really believed that shit, didn't you? This is gonna be fun. Take off your shoes and phones and chuck um in the weeds."

"What? No way, asshole," Helen said.

He put the gun up to her face. "Do it."

They both took their shoes off.

"Good little bitches, now start walking."

45

The Hyenas led Helen and Scares down the wooded path toward the creek. Mark had the pistol pointed at them. It was dark, except for the moonlight peeking through the leaves. Helen was barefoot. The rocky and sharp ground hurt her feet. Scares was still gasping for breath as Mark pushed them forward.

"I'm gonna teach you two a lesson," Mark said as he kicked Scares in the back.

"Stop it, you asshole!" Helen yelled.

"I like your spunk, but that mouth of yours could be put to better use."

"What do you think my dad is gonna do to you?"

"Nothing, 'cause you aren't gonna tell him."

"Maybe, she's right," a pale-looking Eric said.

"Here you go trying to run away again," Mark said. "Maybe, I should shoot you too?"

"Dude, you're going too far," Eric said.

"Shut up! This bitch and her little boyfriend are gonna get dealt," he said, pushing Helen into the water. "You should have never crossed me."

"Hey, look at this," Eric said.

Mark stopped and looked toward the edge of the creek. Caleb Jenkins sat there working on a large clay sculpture of a boy.

"Oh, Clay Boy is here too?" Mark said. "This just keeps getting better and better."

Caleb spun around when he heard Mark's voice.

"The ballgame is starting soon, anyway. We should just go back, or Coach will kill us," Eric said.

"Shut up; I'm just gonna scare them a little," Mark said. He pointed the gun at Helen.

"W-what are you doing?" A wide-eyed Caleb asked.

"Just having some fun with your friends. We are having fun, aren't we, new girl?" Mark said and grabbed her by the hair to pull her close to him.

"Let her g-go."

"Naw, I don't think so. What kind of freaky things does this fucking weirdo do out here? Grab a stick and fuck it up!" he said to Eric.

"What?" a sheepish Eric asked.

"I said mess it up, now!" Mark told Eric and waved the gun at him.

Eric picked up a sharp stick, walked over to the sculpture, and ran the point across its face.

Mark waved the weapon. "More!"

"S-Stop!" Caleb yelled and ran toward Eric.

Mark tripped him.

Eric dug the tip deep into one of its eyes until the stick broke off.

Caleb raised up. His face was smeared with the clay mud that made up this part of the woods. "D-don't!"

Helen lunged at a surprised Mark, and they struggled for control of the gun.

"Stop! You're crazy … I wasn't going to shoot …"

The gun went off.

The two backed away from each other.

Helen looked down at the bullet hole in her left arm near the bicep, took another step back, and collapsed.

"Helen!" Scares rushed to her side. "Oh, shit … she's bleeding bad."

Caleb ran over and bent down beside her.

"Oh, shit! You shot her!" Eric said. He was running his hands through his hair over and over. "We need to get help."

"It was her fault," Mark said, shaking his head.

Caleb looked up at Mark with pure hate in his eyes.

"I'm going to kill you!" He jumped on the lead Hyena, pounding with both fists.

"Get off me!" Mark yelled and smacked Caleb hard across the temple with the gun's butt.

Caleb fell to the ground, blood pouring from his head.

Scares moved toward Mark, but Mark pointed the gun at him. "Stay back! Let's go," he said to Eric.

Back at the creek's edge, Scares was waving his hands in disbelief. "I'm going for help," Scares said. "Just hang in there." He ran down the trail behind Mark and Eric.

Caleb was barely conscious. He crawled over to the feet of the clay boy, and slowly and painfully pulled himself up, so he was eye to eye with his creation. He touched the sculpture's marred cheek, leaving a hand print of fresh blood on it.

"B-best friends," Caleb whispered before falling back to the ground.

The head of the sculpture moved and looked down at Caleb's limp body.

46

When Tina awoke, she was in complete darkness and instantly started gagging and choking in a panic. She calmed herself enough to listen for anyone nearby on the outside, but after several minutes of silence, she started beating and kicking the inside of the trunk as hard as she could, but it got her nowhere. She had been going in and out of consciousness, and now she had begun to hyperventilate but eventually managed to control her breathing again.

She felt around for a flashlight or anything that could produce light. She felt the end of something pointed and cold, a screwdriver, and she started to try and pop the lock, but it took many attempts, but after several minutes, she heard a click and the trunk lid popped open.

"Yes," she whispered in victory as she pulled herself out of the patrol car. She wasn't sure if it was the sheriff who had taken her or someone who had stolen the sheriff's car, but she wasn't going to wait around to find out. She started running as fast as her feet would take her.

47

The baseball stands were nearly full for the big Homecoming game between the Wildcats and the Decatur Bulls, plus the passing of the Diamond Queen crown to a new lucky girl was taking place right after the game.

Coach Darter glanced down at his watch. He was getting a little worried since his star player Mark Mallory and a few of his other starting players hadn't shown up yet. He also saw that Bill Hall wasn't there to raise the flag for the anthem, and he was never late.

Dark clouds gathered on the horizon, and the air felt like rain. Sam picked up his cell phone and dialed home. It rang twice before Marie answered.

"Hello?"

"Hey babe, are you and Helen coming to the game?'

"Helen's not here."

"She on her way?"

"Don't be mad."

"This doesn't sound good," Sam said, shaking his head.

"She was with that boy she met at the video store, She called and said they were looking for Caleb in the woods, but now I can't get a hold of her. It goes straight to voicemail"

"Dammit, I told her to not see him anymore," the pitch of his voice increased as he let out a loud sigh.

"She just wanted to say it in person."

"Yeah, right, and you believed that? I'm gonna call her as soon as I hang up with you."

"Go easy on her, Sam. This move has been a big change. You want me to head up there?"

"Hold off, let me call her first. She might be on her way here."

"Okay. You excited about the big game?"

"Yeah, if I can get all of my players to show up. Hey, I gotta go; love you."

"Love you too, bye."

Coach Darter spotted Mark and Eric come lumbering out of the nearby woods. He raised his arms and whistled to them.

They abruptly stopped and lowered their heads when they saw him. They knew they were busted and started to make their way over. Sam noticed Mark had blood on his shirt.

"What were you two doing in the woods? Is that blood on your shirt?" Coach said with his arms crossed.

Eric looked like he was about to burst into tears as he started to tell what happened, but Mark punched him in the arm and he went silent.

"I asked you a question."

Eric's eyes kept shifting from Coach Darter to Mark.

"Look at me, not him."

"Mark beat up this kid called Scares, and he knocked Caleb Jenkins out. I think he's hurt pretty bad."

"Scares? He the kid that works at the video store?" Sam said, waving his hands.

A teary-eyed Eric nodded.

"Is Helen with him?"

"Yes, sir."

"I swear to God if either of you hurt her, I'm gonna kill you. You're both gonna take me to them." The veins in his neck were throbbing, and he had his finger in Mark's face.

"She's been … sh-shot," Mark said.

"What did you say?" Sam asked wide-eyed.

"It was an accident," Eric added.

Sam's heart lodged itself in his throat. Spots danced before his eyes. The most precious thing in his life was bleeding in the woods, according to these two.

He picked up his cell and dialed 911. "Jesus, pick up!"

"911, what's your emergency?"

"A girl has been shot. She's in the woods next to the middle school ball field. Please hurry," he said and pushed Mark to start walking. "Let's go, start moving."

48

They hadn't been walking down the wooded trail for long before hearing the low rumble of thunder in the far distance. The sun had slipped behind gathering dark clouds, and Mark started complaining about being under trees, fearing a lightning strike.

Sam glanced at his cell. "Dammit, no service.

"It was an accident," Mark said.

"Shut up, Mallory. Where is she?"

"I think it was over there. I can't really remember, Coach," Mark rambled.

"Don't bullshit me, Mallory! Where are …"

The words barely escaped his lips, when he spotted what looked like the body of a young boy. He was partially on the bank of the creek and partially in the water. Sam broke past a wide-eyed Mark and bolted to the side of the injured boy.

"Caleb?"

So many things were rushing through the young principal's head. What if this boy was dead? Had he done enough to stop the bullying that was going on in the school? He reached down to take Caleb in his arms and lifted him from the water. Caleb had lost a lot of blood, and his breathing was shallow.

"Caleb, it's Coach Darter; stay with us. Help should be coming soon."

"Dad?" a weak voice said from behind him.

Sam turned to see Helen lying just a few feet away.

He ran over to her.

"I feel cold," Helen said, staring into space but still managing a smile at the sight of her father. "How's Caleb?"

"Oh, God. I'm going to get help," he said, taking off his baseball jersey and tying it around her arm to make a better tourniquet than the one Scares had made. The spots behind his eyes were growing larger. He gasped for more oxygen and tried to steady himself. He had to save these kids. *Come on, Sam, this is the ninth inning, and you are down two. You need to toughen up. You have to throw strikes.*

Sam jumped up and grabbed Mark. "You little shit! You're going help me get them out of these woods!"

"Wait, what is that? Up in the tree," Eric said.

Coach Darter squinted his eyes and saw something in the treetop. At first, he thought it was Caleb's face, but as the light exposed more of its features, he realized it wasn't him, or even human. It was the face of the clay sculpture, and the absence in its eyes that had been partially reformed by Caleb's offering of blood left Sam speechless. They were as close to pure hate as he'd ever seen.

"My God, what is that?" he mumbled, slack-jawed.

It leaped from one tree limb to the next; it looked like an old stop-motion creature from a Ray Harryhausen B-movie come to life.

It got closer and closer with every leap.

"It's coming for me!" Mark screamed as he pushed past Coach Darter and took off running.

"Wait!" Sam yelled.

Mark Mallory's heart was beating in his throat as he sped past rocks and trees, trying to put as much space as he could between the clay creature and himself. He was almost out of the woods when he tripped over a protruding root and fell to the ground. The fall took his breath out of him and wracked his body with pain, but the steady flow of adrenaline forced him back to his feet to continue his futile escape. His left foot was in excruciating pain.

He felt something watching him from above. He didn't want to look up, but adrenaline-soaked curiosity caused him to crane his head upwards and scan the trees. At first, he saw nothing, but as his eyes adjusted to the diffused light, he saw what he feared was there all along. It was the silhouetted figure of a boy crawling like a spider across the canopy's web of wooden crosses and veins.

Mark lost sight of it. "Oh … shit … shit. I'm s-sorry about picking on Caleb," the king of the Hyenas whimpered.

49

Lois had her hands clasped together tightly. She was kneeling in front of the crucified Jesus that hung just behind the altar in the barn. She hadn't prayed this hard for anything in a long while, but she was praying that her vision of the baseball field and school covered in flames and destruction did not come true.

Her visions were getting more frequent, vivid, and horrible, and she knew that no matter how much she prayed for her gift to be taken away, it wouldn't be, and the visions would always come true. She had often questioned if they even came from God?

The door swung open behind her with only the snap of the latch, and she turned to see her sister Claire standing there. She was in a red dress.

"Claire?"

Lois was once again seven years old, holding onto a doll. Her hair was straight and hung long past the middle of her back. She was on her knees, scribbling furiously on the ground.

"Please save Caleb, Loisy."

She looked up to see someone else standing behind her sister.

"Who's there?" Lois said.

Stepping out from behind Claire was Caleb.

Lois smiled. "Caleb, thank God! Are you okay?"

Caleb didn't smile.

"What's wrong?"

Nestor and his congregation walked into the barn. Nestor was yelling Bible scripture while some of them were carrying torches.

"Don't hurt him!" Lois yelled. Blood was on her hands.

They were all suddenly gone.

Lois turned to see a clay version of Caleb hanging on the cross.

"*And I don't understand why I sleep all day. And I start to complain when there's no rain*," he sang.

"And it rips my life away, but it's a great escape …"

"Escape."

"Escape."

"Escape."

Lois woke up in her bed screaming. She was covered in sweat. Just outside the window a sparrow had lighted on the ledge.

50

The clay boy scurried down the tree to block the path. A terrified Mark closed his eyes and started to pray for anyone to come and save him from this nightmare, but no one could help him. His time had come like Wheeler's Cove's time had come.

The clay boy grabbed Mark by each arm. Its grip was like an iron vice as it dug its fingers into Mark's shoulders.

"Please … don't," he pleaded.

Blood rose to the surface of his skin as the Tulpa grip tightened. The living sculpture moved its powerful hands up to Mark's head. There was the sound of his skull cracking.

The clay automaton stared at the life leaving his best friend's tormentor and then tossed the limp body aside before scurrying up a tree, with the head of Mark Mallory tucked neatly in the crook of its arm.

51

Coach Darter ran with Helen's limp body in his arms. Scares carried Caleb and Eric Frame ran not far behind, looking into the trees for the clay monster.

"We have to hurry," Helen mumbled, barely coherent. She was more worried about Caleb than herself.

"Don't try to speak. You gotta save your energy. We're almost out of the woods. Check and see if you have cell phone reception! I wanna know if that ambulance has arrived," Coach Darter yelled to Eric.

Eric stopped to pull the phone from his pocket and dialed 911. "It's ringing! Hello, I need an ambulance at the Wheeler Middle School's ball field!"

Scares lowered his head to Caleb's chest. "I can't hear him breathing!"

As they broke through the tree line, Sam heard the ambulance and saw the flashing lights pulling up to the home dugout.

Eric Frame was winded and had to stop.

"I can't believe Mark just ran off and left me. What an asshole," he said as he tried to catch his breath. He sat on a fallen tree to regain his wind and saw Mark's face peeking around a tree trunk a few feet away.

"There you are! I thought we were friends?"

Mark just stared at Eric.

"Dude, what's wrong with you?" Eric said, walking toward him. "This is no time to play games. We could be in big trouble if either of them dies. Mark?"

As Eric reached out to Mark, the severed head dropped to the ground and rolled to the toe of Eric's white tennis shoes.

Eric let out a noise like an animal that knows it's about to die. The clay creature clung to the other side of the tree like a cat eyeing its prey.

It grabbed Eric, pulling him up in one quick movement, and then scurried backward up into the foliage of the evergreen like a giant spider that had just caught a fly in its web.

Body parts rained down from above.

The blood-soaked clay boy cocked its ear to the wind. The sound of people and sirens caught its attention. It tossed what remained of Eric to the ground and set out toward the ball to find Caleb.

52

Tina ran through the woods, and as she got closer to the ball field, she could smell smoke. Up ahead, she saw the outline of a person blocking the deer path. They appeared in silhouette, the sun sinking behind their back. At first, she thought it might be the person who had tried to kill her, but as she walked closer, she realized it was a teenage boy.

"Hello?" she asked.

The figure said nothing and walked closer to her.

"Caleb Jenkins, is that you? Thank God you're here! I've been locked inside the trunk of a police car. I know that sounds crazy, but I managed to get out. I think the sheriff may be the Cove Strangler. We n-need to go get someone, and …"

The boy cocked his head, but he didn't move.

"This is serious!" she cried, walking closer to him. "Why aren't you saying anything? Are you still mad about detention?"

Silence.

She started to fidget.

The boy didn't move.

"You're not Caleb. What … are you?"

The clay boy reached into her chest, pulling out her still-beating heart, which it greedily devoured in front of the wide-eyed beauty queen.

"I was … supposed to … pass … my crown … to—," she said, as the last bit of blood pumped through her body.

She fell to the ground, and the last thing she heard was the uproar of what should have been applause coming from the nearby ball field, but it sounded like a group of terrified people.

53

The clouds grew ominous as Sheriff Darter made his way back to his police cruiser from the woods. He cursed when he saw his open trunk. "Dammit!" He looked around the car and back toward the woods and then reached into his car to grab his radio.

"Dispatch, this is the sheriff … you there?"

"This is dispatch; what's up, Marcus?"

"I'm gonna check out the woods for the Jenkins boy one more time before I call it quits today. I'm over at that small patch of woodland that separates Wheeler Middle School from Bill Hall's farm. I shouldn't be out here long."

"Roger, that. The Nashville Local 2 News has been calling all day. They want to know when you're gonna give a statement about the deaths of the Cardin lady and Bill Hall."

"I'll call them when I get time. Put on a pot of coffee. It's gonna be a long night."

"Hey, there was a call for an ambulance at the ball field. Should I send a car?"

"Naw, I'm close. I'll check it out."

"Be careful out there, Sheriff."

"I always am," he whispered and shook his head as he placed the walkie back into the car. He took a large flashlight from his trunk and started down the old deer path toward the creek.

He hadn't walked long when he noticed splotches of blood on the ground.

The sheriff's head shot up at the sound of laughter, and he shone the light toward the dark trees. It seemed to be coming from above him. He kept walking until he reached the water's edge.

Someone was behind him. He pulled out his service pistol and whirled around with his spotlight.

"Who's there? You best just come on out!"

He kept his gun pointed as he backed up.

There was laughter again from up in the trees.

"Caleb, that you?"

Sheriff Darter redirected his flashlight to illuminate the trees on the other side of the creek and then in all directions. As he lowered it, he spotted the body of Tina Rathburn lying on the clay bank, her expression frozen in gaping terror. Her chest was a bloody cavity with her rib cage exposed.

"Goddamn."

More laughter.

"That's real funny. What are you doing out here?"

Silence.

The sheriff gripped his pistol tighter and smiled. "Caleb, I think you might be confused. I can help you."

"Caleb," the voice said from the darkness.

"I think you've had some kind of mental break. I can help you. Just come on over here."

Sheriff Darter heard the cracking of tree limbs high above. He was getting spooked, which he usually never did.

"Now, who are people gonna believe: the town sheriff or a crazy kid that makes shit out of clay? You might as well just come down here and let's work this out."

He put away his pistol and pulled out his murder cord, pulling it taut.

"It's usually not my style to kill men or teenage boys, but I had to make an exception with Bill. He was gonna spill his guts to everyone about our little games."

"You k-killed mother," the distant voice said.

"How do you know that? I hate to be the one to break it to you, but she was nothing but a little whore. She was so much fun to break, and what luck that I found her hitchhiking. I could have killed you too, but killing babies is a little much, even for me.

"Bill and me owned them girls. We still own their souls. Can you believe all this started with a conversation over beers in his barn? What would it feel like to kill someone? And if you are going to kill someone, why not those stuck-up Wheeler Diamond bitches? We buried their bodies under the old farm equipment in his field until we ran out of room. Then we would just dump them beside the freeway. Those whores think they have power over men, but they don't." Sheriff Darter spit on the ground. "Can you believe that I asked out the Diamond Queen when I was in school, and she laughed at me?"

The Sheriff shined his flashlight and noticed the figure of a boy standing to his left.

"There you are. You spooked me, and that never happens. Bill scared real easy. You frightened him with those damn keys. He went on and on about those combine keys that was on his nosy wife's body when she fell down that well. She figured out what Bill and me had been up to. I told him to cement over that thing, but he was a little stubborn and lazy."

He walked toward the boy.

"I'm gonna report back to the station that I found your body not far from where we found Bill Hall. I'll make it look like he killed you and that he killed those girls too all on his own," he said. "Nothing is gonna happen to me, and you wanna know why? 'Cause I'm the goddamn sheriff, that's why. Hell, I'll be a hero."

When he got close enough to the clay boy, he realized it wasn't Caleb.

"Jesus, a clay sculpture? Why is this here?"

The statue lurched to life, grabbing the surprised sheriff by his face.

"What? Help!" the sheriff cried, dropping the flashlight.

The clay boy squeezed until blood ran from the sheriff's ears and eyes. Then it slammed the helpless sheriff's head into a nearby tree over and over until there was nothing left but a bloody mass of pulp.

The clay boy tossed the sheriff's limp body aside and set out to destroy everything in its path to get to his best friend.

54

Sam made it to the clearing and saw the ambulance pulling up near the field. His muscles felt like taffy as he tried to tap any energy reserves he could muster.

"Hang on, baby, Daddy is going to get you to the ambulance. Everything is going to be alright."

Helen felt like a bloody rag doll in his arms. Her breathing was shallow, and he feared the worst.

The closer he got to the school, the field, and the ambulance, the more he noticed large plumes of smoke billowed from behind the hill and poured from the windows of Wheeler Middle School.

People ran from the doors, screaming and crying, covered in blood and soot. The ball field stands were half-filled. People had moved onto the diamond, pushing together like a herd of frightened cattle.

Sam's overwhelmed brain tried to make sense of the chaos. He froze for a moment until his assistant Mary Beth came running. Panic vibrated from her entire body.

"Oh, my God! Is that Helen?"

Her voice didn't register for a moment as everything went mute for Sam. Every person in his life that he was responsible for was in danger. How could he protect his students and his faculty when he couldn't even protect his daughter?

"Sam!" Mary Beth yelled again and grabbed his shoulder to shake him. "You need to snap out of it. We need you!"

"What's happening?" Coach Darter snapped back to action.

"There's a boy — I don't know who it is, but he's killing people. I think it may be a shooting, but I'm not sure. It's absolute chaos in there."

A tense Scares stood nearby with a limp Caleb in his arms.

"Take Helen and put her inside the ambulance, Scares. Do the same with Caleb and lock the doors until the police get here. I talked to my wife, she is supposed to be here too. Have you seen her? And where are the police?"

Mary Beth lowered her head. Her eyes started to blink over and over.

"What?"

"She thought Helen was inside the school. She went in to find her, I tried to talk her out of it."

"Dammit!" He headed toward the school.

"Where are you going? You can't go in there!" she pleaded.

"I have to! Just make sure my daughter is safe." He went to the back of the ambulance, grabbed an oxygen mask, and then raced into the chaos beyond the front doors.

An out-of-breath Dr. Dorjee tried to stop him at the entry.

"Principal Darter?"

"I don't have time to talk. Just get to the ball field. It's safe there."

"Wait, I'm Caleb Jenkins's therapist. I know what's in there causing this."

Sam stopped in his tracks. "Then what the hell are you waiting for? Tell me!"

"You might find this hard to believe, but that is Caleb in there. I mean, sort of …"

"Caleb is in that ambulance. What are you talking about?"

"This is going to sound crazy, but it's the truth. He created something in his imagination called a Tulpa. He made it to take away the pain in his life that he could not. He built a clay body for it to inhabit, and then he brought that body to life with mental powers that he didn't realize he possessed. Legends have called it a golem, but it's like a robot programmed to destroy everything that has ever thought to hurt Caleb. I know this all sounds absolutely nuts, but you need to trust me."

Sam was a practical man, but something in the doctor's eyes made him listen. "You expect me to believe this?" he asked, pushing past the doctor.

Dr. Dorjee shook his head, gasping for air.

"Wait … I can prove it! Look at the footage of this girl. She was like Caleb. She also made a Tulpa. We need to take Caleb to face this thing. He's the only one who can get rid of it, but doing so killed Bethany."

The doctor's persistence made Sam look at the camera. As he watched, his eyes grew wider and wider.

"Is this real?"

Dorjee placed his hand on Sam's shoulder.

"This thing will kill everyone in there unless we stop it, but we must have Caleb's help."

"He's in the ambulance. I'm not sure if he can even walk, much less battle a monster."

"He has to try. It's the only way to stop this destruction."

Dorjee and Coach Darter ran back to the ambulance. Sam knocked on the doors for them to open, and once they did, he picked up a limp Caleb, who was now awake and reached over and gave Helen a kiss.

"You keep her safe, you hear me?" he said to Scares.

"Yes, sir," Scares said, with his chin up. "I won't let anything happen to her."

"Okay, let's do this, Dorjee," Sam said as they raced toward the school.

55

Coach Darter held a barely conscious Caleb in his arms as he and Dr. Dorjee made their way down the smoke-filled halls. Sam noticed a glass case holding a fire extinguisher and oxygen masks inside.

"Break it! Grab a mask! We'll put it on Caleb, too," Sam said.

Dorjee broke the glass with his elbow and grabbed the mask and the fire extinguisher. "Wait, what about you?"

"I'll be fine."

Dorjee placed the oxygen mask over Caleb's face and his own, before they continued down the long hallway toward the gymnasium.

"Why are we going this way?" Dorjee asked.

"It's the designated place to go if there's a shooting or any kind of attack on the school."

They were near the gymnasium when they saw the disfigured bodies of several students and faculty members lying on the floor of their classrooms.

Lexi had had her arms ripped from their sockets, and her cell phone was in her mouth. Others lay beside her like broken store mannequins.

Dorjee nearly puked at the gruesome sight but managed to hold himself together when he heard a shrill scream. It came from behind the double red-painted doors that led to the basketball courts.

"Through here! Hang in there, little man!" Sam shouted.

"Are you getting tired?"" Dorjee asked Sam.

"My shoulder is hurting a little, but I'm okay."

They burst through the doors and into a flame-filled Hell.

Searing heat filled the court, spreading from the cafeteria kitchens. Sam could make out what he thought were a few students on the floor near the portable practice goals. They fought through small pockets of snapping flames until they reached the bodies.

Sam had to adjust his eyes to see behind the wild flames. Hate-filled eyes glared down at him from the top of the wooden bleachers. The creature had swelled in size, and the expression on its face had grown even crueler, demonic.

The monster jumped down from the bleachers and headed directly for them.

Right before it attacked Sam, it stopped and looked at Caleb.

"It doesn't want to hurt Caleb," Dorjee said.

The insatiable golem backed up into the fire. Its clay body started to turn black from the flames licking all over it.

Caleb screamed over the growl of the fire. The connection between him and Gren was now complete, and the pain that his creation felt, he also felt.

A piece of flaming ceiling dropped, putting a barrier between them and the creature.

Barry sprayed the entire contents of the fire extinguisher, but it did little to stop the raging fire. "It's too hot in here. Let's go back into the hallway!" he yelled.

"I need to find my wife!" Sam yelled, scanning the smoke-filled court while searing heat burned his exposed skin. He knew that Caleb couldn't take much more of this. He nodded, and they turned back toward the double doors.

They were now in the smoke-filled, slightly cooler hallway and headed back toward the front doors.

Sam Darter stopped and handed Caleb to Dorjee. "I'm not leaving without Marie! Take him and go!"

"I can walk," Caleb said.

"Okay," Sam said and sat him down.

"You gotta leave with us," Dorjee said. "Wait, who's that?"

Sam turned to see a woman lying in the middle of the hall. When he got closer, he realized that it was his wife. She had succumbed to the smoke but was still alive.

"Thank God, Marie!" Sam said and picked her up into his arms.

"I've got Caleb! We can't face Gren here," Dorjee said.

"Helen. Where's Helen?" Marie asked.

"She's safe outside. I'm taking you to her."

They sprinted and saw the exit ahead, but the clay boy, swathed in fire, was barreling down the hall behind them.

"Jesus, run!" Sam said.

Everything seemed to be moving in slow motion for Sam; as they reached the doors, a small black dot in his vision grew into a large hole, one that suddenly enveloped him. He began to lose consciousness and fell to his knees, but still managed to hold Marie. He could see Barry yelling at him to get up, but he couldn't hear anything. Barry placed Caleb just outside the doors and went back to help Sam with Marie. "I've got her. Just get yourself to safety."

Coach Darter managed to stand and limp into the rain. Dark clouds had blotted out the moon, and a storm brewed on the horizon.

The last thing Sam remembered was laying Marie on the pavement and telling her he loved her.

56

Outside, the cold rain woke Caleb to a throbbing pain in his chest. His vision was blurry, but he could make out the EMTs helping Barry, along with Helen's mom. He also saw his worried aunt and uncle standing not far away. He heard Aunt Lois saying the Lord's Prayer over and over again as tears poured down her cheeks.

"This is all Caleb's doing, isn't it? That boy was sent by the Devil!" Nestor said.

Dark clouds swirled above the ball field. Lois's nightmare vision was coming true, but only she knew how it ended.

"What's happening?" Nestor yelled. "Was this in your drawing?"

She turned to her husband with fire in her eyes. "Shut up, Nestor!

"You hid this from me." Nestor stepped back and lowered his head. "I knew that these powers of yours were never from God. They are from the Devil, and so is that little bastard nephew that came into our lives. I should have never let it happen."

Lois turned and slapped him. "You are a fraud and a scarred little man. Caleb is the only thing that matters to me."

Caleb's entire body started to shake. He could feel that Gren was close.

The clay boy busted through the glass and steel portals of the front doors and out into the parking lot. He noticed Caleb and marched toward him.

Lois stepped between Caleb and the creature. "Stay away from him; he's just a boy."

The creature lunged toward her.

"N-no!" Caleb said.

Gren stopped.

She turned to Caleb and took him into her arms. "I love you. I always have," she said and kissed him.

Dr. Dorjee ran to her and pulled her back. "You must go to safety. Only Caleb can stop it."

She moved to the side as the doctor grabbed Caleb by the shoulder.

"Caleb, listen to me. You need to banish Gren in your mind. You must stop thinking about him. He doesn't exist."

"He's my f-friend. My b-best friend."

"No, he's not your friend. He's the hate and fear that is inside you. He's not your friend!"

"He's the only o-one that has n-never hurt me."

"Your aunt hasn't hurt you. I haven't hurt you."

The wind howled, and a strong gust knocked Caleb off his feet into Barry's arms.

The clay boy moved toward them.

"Come on!" Barry pleaded banged on the doors to the back of the ambulance.

Scares opened them and they both got inside, and Dorjee pulled them close behind them.

Helen lay on a stretcher behind them. She was hooked up to life-saving equipment but needed to get to a hospital soon.

"You must decide that Gren does not exist and never has. You have to do this, or he will kill everyone around you."

"But h-he only wants to p-protect me."

Outside the ambulance, the clay boy had almost reached them.

Dorjee climbed into the front seat and turned the ignition, but the engine only sputtered.

"You've got to be kidding me!"

The ambulance jolted back and forth, knocking Dorjee halfway into the passenger seat. He rose to look directly into the eyes of the clay boy, standing just outside the driver's side window. The creation lifted the front end of the vehicle and slammed it back down. The strong impact caused the keys to fall to the floorboard. Barry reached under the seat, trying to retrieve them.

The clay boy walked around to the back and pulled the doors open.

Helen screamed.

"Gotcha!" Barry said as he grabbed the keys, stuck them back into the ignition, and turned them.

The engine cranked and sputtered.

A funnel cloud touched down in the nearby clearing. Wind and rain were tossing debris everywhere.

"Ca-aleb?" the clay boy said.

Caleb stepped out of the ambulance. "S-stop."

"Caleb, what are you doing? Get back in the ambulance!" Barry yelled.

"No, this is my f-fault," he repeated as he stepped out the recently opened doors to face his creation.

The rain poured as the tornado roared like a freight train.

Caleb heard the muted screams of Aunt Lois and Barry behind him. They were screaming at him to get back inside, but he knew the clay boy would not hurt him because it *was* him. It was his hate. It was his fear. It was his loneliness, and the doctor was right; only Caleb could stop Gren. He understood this now.

From the school, he heard another voice yelling his name. It was a wind-battered Sam. "Caleb, you need to run. Just run!"

Caleb ignored them as he approached Gren, now burnt and blackened. He looked on the outside how Caleb had always felt on the inside. The torrent of water caused the creature's shoulders to sag. It had grown from feeding off Caleb, but its damaged knees bent under its weight, and it slumped down, coming face-to-face with Caleb.

The rain fell harder.

"You need to s-stop. You're hurting p-people. They don't understand what they do. They never do." Caleb caressed Gren's face. "Please g-go. I don't b-believe in you anymore."

The creature cocked its head like a dog that couldn't understand why its owner no longer wanted it.

"You have to go back into the d-darkness now. I needed you, but I don't need you anymore."

"No, Gren want to stay. Best friends. We play in woods." This came out of Caleb's mouth, but it was distorted and guttural, but the voice changed back to soft when it was Caleb's turn to speak.

"N-no," Caleb said, as his eyes filled with tears.

"We go together, now? Best friends forever," Gren said, extending a blackened clay hand to Caleb.

"No, we c-can't go together."

"Gren not want to go."

The rain poured over the creature's face giving the illusion of tears coming from its eyes.

"Goodbye," Caleb said.

The clay boy became motionless as the spirit that animated it drained away.

Caleb pulled a clay sparrow from his pocket. He sat it on the Gren's shoulder and slumped against his creation, before closing his tear-filled eyes. The roaring funnel cloud in the distance turned toward the nearby woods, and the wind around them faded, until the only thing Caleb could hear was the steady sound of falling rain.

Acknowledgements

Clay Boy would not be possible without the support from some amazing people. I would first like to thank Heather and S.D. Vassallo from Brigids Gate Press for taking a chance on my novel. This book would not be possible without their hard work and professionalism along the editors and artists that assist them. I would like to extend my gratitude to Patricia Feinberg Stoner and her husband Patrick of Perdisma Editing for helping to get this novel into shape. They know my strengths and weaknesses and are integral in helping my writing to be the best it can be.

I am over the Moon with Elizabeth Leggett's phenomenal cover art that perfectly captures the mood of the novel. As with all books, a cover is a person's first contact with a book and is so important on whether they choose to take a deeper look. I hope you can appreciate the power that her artistic contribution brings to this project.

Lastly, but not last in importance, is my family and fellow writing community. Where I am today is no mere coincidence, but is a collection of support and encouragement from over the years. My mother Clarice Smith who has literally been there from day one. I love you. My partner in life and crime Chloe Gardner and her family that have accepted me as a part of their family. Thanks to Gregg Stewart, a great writer and human, for reading Clay Boy and giving such good notes. My upmost thanks to Douglas Draa for giving me my first break in writing, and to such writing legends who have not only written stories that made me want to become a writer, but they have also been kind enough to answer my questions and offer encouragement. I truly appreciate Joe R. Landsdale for being so kind and being a gentleman whenever I had the opportunity to meet or chat with him. And a special thanks to my eleventh grade English teacher Von Joy Holland Lacy that took the time to tell me that I had talent. You have no idea how much those words meant to me.

ABOUT THE AUTHOR

Craig E Sawyer is an American writer known for horror, western, sci-fi, and crime, and is a direct descendant of the McCoy family that famously feuded against the Hatfield's over a stolen pig. He has been published by Timber Ghost Press, Horror Smith Publishing, Quill & Crow Publications, Brigids Gate Press, Shotgun Honey, Weirdbook, Schlock Publications, Crystal Lake Press, Nightmare Press, Monkeys Fighting Robots, Levy-Gardner-Laven Productions, and Skull Dust Press. He is the creator of the horror/adventure comic *The Forbidden Museum*, and the RPG sci-fi board game *Escape from Dulce*. Craig traveled much of the United States, eventually settling on the West Coast, and before becoming a writer he worked as a bartender, roofer, carpet weaver, bouncer, and actor.

Content Warnings

Animal death
Bullying

More From Brigids Gate Press

In 1926, nine-year-old Rosalyn invents a new game to play with the girls she shares a dormitory with in the Hawthorne House Orphanage. Revolving around a Royal Court, their make-believe game quickly becomes a way to gain some measure of control in their unhappy lives. But when the rules start changing and the stakes start rising, nothing is safe, and Rosalyn finds that she's willing to get her hands dirty in order to be the Queen.

Rosalyn will do *whatever* it takes to wear the crown.

All that's left is to take it.

The story of a girl begins with a boy. On Christmas morning, 1982, nine-year-old Jude Bendz survives the shocking and mysterious death of his twin sister, Mary. Bewildered by grief, he is comforted when, miraculously, Mary's ghost appears, her spirit quickly informing a series of fantastic apparitions through which her life – and death – come into clearer focus. Problems soon arise, however, when his sister, promising salvation, places him at the center of a wide, yet narrowing plot that increasingly puts his life in mortal danger.

A tragic accident, shrouded in mystery, leads to a family reunion in the hidden village of Little Hatchet, located in the smothering shadow of GodBeGone Wood, the home of the mythical Woodcutter and Grandma. Alec Eades rediscovers his bond with GodBeGone Wood and the future his father agreed to years ago as nefarious landowner Oliver Hayward schemes to raise money for the village by re-enacting part of the Woodcutter legend. Old wounds are reopened and ties of blood and friendship are tested to the extreme when the Woodcutter is summoned and Grandma returns.

According to Dante, a **sin** is the misdirection of love-the human will, or essentially, the direction of our beings. Love the Sinner is an examination of just how those sins can kaleidoscope into **horrific** consequences creating a distorted and **deadly** landscape. These stories stand stark before you in full glaring misstep and **macabre** to show the human psyche in all its twisted reality. From grief and its rage to medical meddling to ensure a new world order to bloody **revenge** within a quantum leap, these stories seek to solidify one absolute truth: man is the scariest **monster**.

Visit our website at: www.brigidsgatepress.com

Printed in the USA
CPSIA information can be obtained
at www.ICGtesting.com
LVHW041820221223
767233LV00002B/155